# Praise For Rick Collignon

"Collignon delivers hi[...]
of magical realism wit[...]
humor, and bracingly i[...]

—*Publisher's Weekly*

"Graceful descriptions and inventive
Southwestern surrealism."

—*The New York Times Book Review*

"Mr. Collignon has created
a distinct and meaningful world."

—*Atlantic Monthly*

"Especially reminiscent of García Márquez's
magical realism ... Settle back and thoroughly
enjoy the journey."

—*Library Journal*

"Evocative...Collignon pays homage to the
power of storytelling."

—*Booklist*

"Intriguing. Compelling. Collignon's characters
are masterfully drawn, as is his rendering of the
stark New Mexico landscape, with its
harsh unforgiving climate."

—*The San Diego Union-Tribune*

"A real gem...beautiful and moving."

—John Nichols, author of *The Milagro Beanfield War*

# LOST IN A
# PLACE SO SMALL

RICK COLLIGNON

## Also by Rick Collignon

*The Journal of Antonio Montoya*

*Madewell Brown*

*A Santo in the Image of Cristóbal García*

*Perdido*

# LOST IN A
# PLACE SO SMALL

## RICK COLLIGNON

AN IMPRINT OF BOWER HOUSE

DENVER

*Printed in Canada*
*Designed by Margaret McCullough  margaretmccullough.com*
*Cover Illustration based on the work of Gustave Baumann: American printmaker and painter, and one of the leading figures of the color woodcut revival in America.*

Library of Congress Control Number: 2019957297
Paperback ISBN: 978-1-942280-66-8
Ebook ISBN: 978-1-942280-67-5

10  9  8  7  6  5  4  3  2  1

TO MILO AND JULIAN

# ONE

**WILL SAWYER HAD LIVED** in the village of Guadalupe for more than thirty years when one day, near the end of a warm, dry September, he found the bones of a child buried in the wall of the old García house. He found them down low in the wall, just a couple of feet above the floor line and beneath a layer of mud plaster that he'd pulled away from the adobe. It was late afternoon when this happened, and he was alone. All the windows and doors in the house were wide open, and had been all day, but even with a slight breeze moving through the three small rooms, the place was still dark and stank of mildew and rotted dirt and old dust that had lain untouched for years.

At first, Will thought that what he'd found was a chance placement of sticks, or maybe the smooth, narrow stones he sometimes found at the river. But when he looked closer, he could see how they bulged out slightly from the surface and fanned apart equally as if placed there for some purpose. He squatted down, grimacing at the pull in his knees that had been growing worse and worse over the past few years, and brushed away the loose dirt and bits of straw with the flat of his hand.

"What is this?" he said, softly.

They looked almost like thin, yellowed sticks that had been cut and peeled from willow branches. He traced one of them with his fingertip, his nail scraping until it met with a slight ridge halfway along its length. He moved awkwardly onto his hands and knees and, squinting, brought his face close and blew on the surface until it was clean. Then he angled his body off to the side so that the light coming in the window behind him fell on the wall. He could see them better now, and, as if the temperature in the room had suddenly plunged, a chill ran up his spine and touched the back of his neck.

"Jesus," he whispered.

Just a foot away and half buried in the adobe were what looked like the bones of four small fingers.

The old house sat up on a slope at the far southeast edge of the village. It had been abandoned for decades, and the only things around it were patches of pale, sparse grass and sagebrush that grew wild and thick and gnarled. Standing alone just a little ways above the house was a tall piñon tree. The ground beneath it was bare dirt. Its trunk was scarred deep from deer and porcupines, the lower branches cut away. Two frayed ropes hung from an upper limb, as if there had once been a swing, although there was such a lonely, deserted feel to the place that it was hard for Will to imagine anyone up here swinging, let alone a child. Beyond the piñon, sage ran all the way up to a thick border of dwarf piñon and juniper trees. A quarter mile farther up, the foothills began to climb. Will didn't know much about the old house, only that it had supposedly been in the García family forever and that the owner, an old woman named Manuela García, lived just down the hill.

Manuela García had gotten Will's name a few weeks before from her neighbor, Bernabe Medina, who, like her, was old and lived alone with just his few head of sheep. He lived a half mile down the road, and she had walked that distance in the early evening when the day had begun to cool.

When Bernabe had come to the door and seen who it was, he'd kept quiet for a few seconds, and then nodded and spoke her name and stepped outside, closing the door behind him. She told him she was looking for someone to work a little on her house and had come here to see if he knew of anyone who could help her. She said that she would prefer it was not someone from this village as the man she'd hired a few years before, that Cisneros boy, always stunk of beer and was too stupid to leave alone.

From inside the house, Bernabe could hear the low drone of his television telling of bad news in the world, and out in the pen by the edge of his field his sheep began to call for him. Bernabe, who had barely glanced at his neighbor while she'd asked this favor of him, finally looked at her.

He had not seen her in years, and he could see that, like him, she had grown old. Then it went through his mind that he had yet to feed his sheep and that his dinner dishes were still unwashed and that here he was talking to Manuela García who his late wife, Pelimora, had never liked, let alone trusted.

"I know a man," he said, more to have her leave than anything else. "He helped me with the shingles on my roof. He lives here, but he's not from this village." Then he stepped by her. "His name's Will Sawyer." And without looking back at her, he said, "My sheep are calling for me."

Now, as she sat across from this man who had come to see her, Manuela could see that he was not what she had expected. He was older than she'd thought he would be, close to fifty or maybe even a few years older. He was tall and thin. His skin was weathered and lined, and there was a tired look to his eyes.

His hair was a little too long, and there was more gray than brown in it. He sat across from her with one leg stretched out, leaning back in his chair as if he didn't care too much about anything.

"Well," he said to her. "So you called me."

"Yes," she said. "I did. But let me get you a little coffee first," and without waiting for him to answer she went to the stove and poured coffee into a cup and brought it to the table. She placed it in front of him, and then smoothed her dress and sat back down.

"It's not this house I need help with," she said. "It's the one up the hill. My grandfather's house."

They were sitting in her kitchen. There was a small window over the sink that faced east and out it, some one hundred yards away, Will could see the old house.

The sun was reflecting off the three windows, and it surprised him a little that there was still glass in the twisted frames. He could see that the plaster on the outside walls was long gone and that all there was to the roof was bare, gray wood. He knew the floors would be dirt and the inside walls badly eaten away by roof leaks.

"I've gotten old," Manuela went on. "And I'm trying to put some things in order before I die. One of them is my grandfather's house." She folded her hands together and smiled, "I want you to fix it for me."

Will had gotten calls like this before, from some viejo who felt bad asking more favors from their relatives and thought it might be easier on the whole family to just pay someone, even if it was someone they didn't know so good. Will would have a beer with them or a cup of coffee and when they finally got around to what they wanted done and heard what it would cost, they'd spit out a breath and shake their heads and tell him they'd had no idea such a little job would be so much, and that they would have to think about it for a little while before they decided. And after he was gone, they'd call their brother or their son or a second cousin and ask if they wouldn't mind coming over to nail on a few shingles or put putty around the windows or fix the fence so the neighbors' cows would stay out.

Will looked out the window. What he saw up the hill was a mess, and he wondered why of all the things this old woman might choose to do before she died she had chosen this one. He thought that even if the place was fixed up, plastered on the outside, a new roof, the inside cleaned out, there would still be no electricity, no water, and even if he cut in a road, it would turn to mud every time it rained. And the cost of everything that needed to be done would surely be beyond this old woman.

"What did you have in mind?" he asked, looking back at her. He reached for his coffee and took a sip. There was a burnt, sour taste to it, and he wondered when she had made it.

"I want it to be the way I remember it as a young girl," she said.

"What about power and water?"

"No," she said, shaking her head. "That's not important to me."

Will didn't say anything for a few seconds. He just sat there, his hand still wrapped around his coffee cup. And then he drew his leg up and pushed forward a little in his chair.

"I'm not sure if you want to think about this," he said, "but it would be easier and a lot cheaper to just tear the place down. It wouldn't take much. It's leaning bad enough as it is. Maybe you could get some neighbors to help you out, or family. You could haul away the trash, smooth out the dirt, and then there'd be nothing blocking the view of the foothills."

Manuela stared back at him and then closed her eyes. Her smile got a little tighter, and she was quiet for so long that Will wondered if she'd drifted off, wondered if she'd heard a word he'd said.

When she finally opened her eyes, she said, "I don't care about the foothills, and I have no family left in this village to ask. Besides, I've already thought about this house looking the way it once did."

Again, Will looked out the window. The sun was beginning to set, and there was a burnt cast to the light, making everything look softer than it was. A part of him thought it might not be so bad working up there. No one would bother him, and the job was pretty straightforward. But another part of him knew it was a waste of time and a waste of the old woman's money. Maybe this was important to her now, but after she was dead no one would care about the old house. And even if it looked a little better, it would still be an abandoned shell stuck out in the middle of nothing. He was a little surprised that the old woman didn't see that.

"I don't know," he said. "I'll have to think about it. But I do know that it's going to cost a lot more than it'll ever be worth."

"That's not your concern," she said. "Your concern should be making an old woman happy. Besides, I have more money than I need."

"I think the problem," Will said, and he smiled, "is me taking it from you."

Manuela sat looking at him for a few seconds, and then she brought her hands to the table. They were shaking a little, and she clasped them together.

"Would you like some more coffee?" she asked.

"No," Will said. "I'm fine." He picked up the cup and finished it off. He could taste coffee grounds in his mouth. He thought that he would stay for a few minutes more and then leave.

"Are you hungry?" she asked. "I have meat in the refrigerator. I can make you a sandwich."

"No," Will said, holding up a hand. "I need to be home soon. But thank you."

6

"Let me ask you something then," Manuela said. "Do you think I had you come here just to drink a cup of coffee with me?"

And just like that, although the tone of her voice hadn't changed, Will knew that somewhere in this conversation with this old woman he had missed something and he had a feeling that he was about to find out what it was.

"No," he said, looking at her. "That's not what I think."

"Did you think we were just going to have a little talk, and then you would leave me to myself, like I was a foolish old woman who was wasting your time?"

"No," he said. "I didn't think that either," although in truth, that had been more or less exactly what he'd been thinking.

"Good," she said. She leaned back in her chair and smiled. "Then maybe we can start over again. Just when do you think you could begin this work?"

For a moment, Will didn't say anything. He just stared back at her. She was sitting up straight, her hands back in her lap. She was a small, slight woman with long, thinned-out gray hair that fell below her shoulders. Her skin was pale and meshed with fine lines that crisscrossed her face and threaded down her neck. Her eyes were dark and set deep, a faint scar ran from the corner of one eye and down her cheek. She moved her head up and a little to one side, as if aware that he was staring at her. It struck him that she had been beautiful once, and he chased the thought away.

"You don't want to hear what I have to say, do you?" he asked.

"No," she said. "I already heard what you had to say. All I want is for you to help me. There is no one else in this village I can ask."

"I'll tell you what I can do then," he said. "I'll think about this for a few days, and then I'll get back to you."

"No," Manuela said, sharply. "I don't want to wait a few days. I've been waiting my whole life to do this. I want you to say yes now."

Will took in a deep breath and let it out slowly. He thought that this old woman was never going to give up and that it was time to end it so that he could leave. "Then I'm sorry," he said to her. "I don't think this job is right for me. I think you should get someone else."

Manuela leaned forward a little over the table. "I was told," she said, her voice low and suddenly harsh, "that you have been in this village a long time. That you married a woman from here and have two young daughters who are part of this place now. I also heard that you know some of the old stories. Stories that most people have forgotten or have never heard. That's what my grandfather's house is. It's one more story for you to have."

Will was having a hard time believing what he was hearing. He leaned back in his chair and reached for a cigarette. Then he dropped his hand and grinned. He knew what she was doing. He just didn't know why she was going to all the trouble. He wondered what it would be like to be married to this woman.

"Who told you all that?" he asked.

Manuela pulled back from the table. "It's not hard to hear things in this village," she said. "Even if you're an old woman who lives alone. You've lived here long enough to know that. Besides, what I said is true, isn't it?"

"Some of it," Will said, letting it go. "But just because I've been told a few things about this village doesn't mean I need to take a job to hear more. After all, they're just stories. And I didn't get the feeling that you asked me here to tell me some more."

"I plan on paying you, también," Manuela said.

Will shook his head and glanced out the window. The old house was in shadows now, and he thought that for all her talk about her grandfather's house, all he'd ever find up there would be pack rats and black widows. What the hell, he thought. It's her money, and I've done all I can to change her mind. On top of that, work had been slow and winter wasn't far off.

"You don't have anyone who can help you with this?" he asked, looking back at her.

"No," she said, and in that moment she knew she had won this first little battle with him. "I already told you that, but you didn't listen."

"All right," he said, holding up both his hands. "I'll help you with this. But I've got a few things to finish up before I can start. I think I can get over here sometime next week."

"Next week will be fine," Manuela said. "But before you leave, I want to tell you how my grandfather's house once was."

"No," Will said, thinking that it was about time he said no to something this old woman wanted. "That can wait. It'll take some time just to tear the place apart and clean it out. You can tell me later. Besides, I think we should take this one step at a time and see what happens."

"That is a good idea, hijo," Manuela said, smiling." I knew I didn't make a mistake with you."

Will grunted. He pushed back his chair and stood up. He felt as if he'd been in this house for a long time. "I'll call you next week," he said.

"I know you will," she said, standing up slowly. She went over to the window and drew the curtains closed. The room was nearly dark now, and as Will turned to leave he heard her say softly, "Thank you, hijo."

That morning, the morning of the day Will Sawyer found the bones of a child buried in the wall of the old García house, began just like any other day on any other jobsite. He drove up to Manuela's house just after dawn and parked beneath a large cottonwood tree that stood beside a dry irrigation ditch. When he climbed out of his pickup, he saw the old woman standing just outside her door. And he realized the sight of her waiting for him didn't surprise him.

"You've come," she said. She was wearing a nightgown that hung low on her shoulders and fell to her knees. Her legs were bone white and thin.

"Yes," Will said. "I did."

"I won't bother you then," she said. "I'll let you get to your work."

"I appreciate that," he said, and they both smiled. When she turned to go back inside, Will grabbed his tool belt and a flat shovel out of the bed of the pickup and walked up the hill to the old house.

The first thing he did when he got there was walk around the place. There was a portal running the length of the back where someone once would sit in the shade and look out at the foothills. The post holding it up at the far corner had rotted away, causing the eave to sag so low that it almost touched the ground. There was one door leading inside, and it, too, was boarded up. There were bits of broken glass and rusted out cans and pieces of rotted roofing paper scattered about, but not much else that Will could see.

After circling the house once, he pulled the boards off the doors with the claw of his hammer, and then shoved them and all the windows wide open, turning his head at the stench that rushed out at him. Then he found a place to sit down against the south wall and stretched out his legs. He poured a cup of coffee from his thermos and lit a cigarette and sat there figuring he'd let the place air out for a little while before going inside.

The sun had just risen above the foothills, and there was a slight haze of dust in the air. It hadn't rained since late July, and there was a dry, sad look to the piñon and juniper farther up the slope. The sagebrush all around the house was dusty, a brittle feel to the branches. One of the frayed ropes hanging from the piñon tree was moving slightly, as if a breeze had caught it or a bird had flown too close. Will watched it until it stilled and then glanced down the hill.

He could see movement inside the kitchen window of Manuela's house and wondered whether she had just pulled open the curtains to let in the day or if she'd been standing there all along, watching.

"I don't remember what's in my grandfather's house," she had told him. "I haven't been up there in so long, and you know how people in this village are about taking things. But I don't think there is one thing in it I want. Just make a big pile somewhere and we can worry about it later."

He smoked another cigarette, and then pushed dirt over the butts, capped his thermos, and stood up. He brushed the dirt off the back of his pants.

"All right," he said to no one. "Let's take a look at this place."

It was cool and, even with the door and window open, dark inside. There was a nearly overwhelming odor of rot and wet dirt and decay, as if something might have died not so long ago. A haze of dust motes hung in the air where sunlight came through the cracks in the wood roof. Across the room was a square of light from the open window, and through it Will could see Manuela's house and the cottonwoods beyond it. He reached in his back pocket and pulled out a bandana and tied it around his nose and mouth. Then, moving his hand through the thin strands of spider webs that spanned the open doorway, he stepped inside.

The room was a mess. There were broken wood chairs in the center of it and filthy blankets and old clothing wadded up and strewn about. Against the far wall was a narrow, steelframed bed with coiled springs. Loose nests from pack rats were woven in the springs and curled down to the floor. The wires were broken and crusted white, and now Will could catch the stale stench of urine. Across from it, in the corner just beside him, was a rusted-out woodstove. The stovepipe and top grates were gone, the dim shadows of ashes and charred pieces of wood still inside. The floor was hard packed dirt. The walls were mud plastered. Most of it had fallen to the floor, and what hadn't had pulled away from the adobe and was streaked with white mold from roof leaks.

He didn't know what to think. It looked as if someone had periodically visited the place and trashed it for some reason. He didn't know if the old woman's grandfather had been the last person in this house or if there had been others that Manuela didn't even know about. She'd even been vague about when she'd last been here. And, looking around, he thought he too might be okay with forgetting about what was in this place. He pressed the bandana tighter against his face and walked around the debris and through a narrow archway that led to the middle room of the house.

It was empty, or nearly so. The walls and the floor were bare. There was a thick glaze of dusty cobwebs where the wall met the roof, and on the underside of the roof boards were old scars, as if sparrows had once nested there. Above Will's head were the swollen, bloated hives from yellow jackets, paper thin and torn and lifeless. A rag hung from a nail on one side of the window, like it had once been used to cover the glass. Will thought he could make out threads from embroidery woven into it, but it was too filthy and the light was too dim for him to be sure. The room was smaller than the other, and he had a feeling that for some reason it had been kept clean purposely, as if whoever had lived here had lived only in the other two rooms. He pulled the bandana away from his face a little. Even the air tasted cleaner.

As he turned to look into the last room, his foot struck something lying on the floor. He watched it hit against the wall and then roll a few inches back toward him. He stepped over to it, stooped down, and picked it up.

It was a marble, something a kid might have. Will rubbed it clean with his fingers. It was pale white and swirled with gray. He glanced around to see if there were more, but all he could see was the flat surface of the mud floor pocked here and there from water.

"What are you doing here?" he said, softly, looking down at it. Again, he rubbed his fingers over it. And then, grunting, he slid it into his pocket and went into the last room of the house.

There was a table in the middle of the room. It looked like oak with a wide surface and thick, heavy legs, and the thought went through Will's mind that it must have been a bitch to have carried it all the way up the hill. The surface of it was littered with dirt and dust and a thick layer of rodent droppings. A large square of rotted linoleum lay on the floor, and the center of it was slightly humped where the bare ground beneath it rose. A stack of rough shelving that must have at one time stood against the far wall was thrown down, some of the shelves splintered. A cookstove stood beside the window. The top grates were missing, and the doors to the oven and warming oven hung open. Empty, flat tins that had once held meat were thrown about, along with broken whiskey bottles and beer cans and more clothing and a shrunken, twisted leather boot and the faded cover of a book and blackened stones that looked as though they had gone through a fire and empty shotgun shell casings and broken pieces of wood and what looked like a smashed kerosene lamp, and who knew what else. It was as big a mess as Will had found in the first room he'd gone into. But there was one thing different about it. In this room the walls were covered with crosses.

They hung on all four walls and above the doorway and the archway behind where Will was standing. They hung above the window and down close to the floor. There must have been hundreds of them. Some were made from peeled sticks tied together with frayed string or leather. Others were limbs from sagebrush, their leaves dried and curled, still on the branches. There were crosses of flat boards and rusted metal and somewhere Will could tell the wood had been carved. Some were so small they looked like they'd been made from twigs, and others looked like limbs cut from cedar trees.

And as Will stood in the middle of this room gazing about him, what struck him was that Manuela García must have known these things were here. And if she did, why hadn't she told him? He remembered what she'd said when they talked on the phone just a few days before.

"It shouldn't take you so long, hijo," she'd told him, her voice low and distant. "After all, what could be in a house that has sat empty for so long?"

And her words would come back to him again later. The moment he uncovered the four small bones in the wall.

# TWO

✤ WILL WAS STANDING OUTSIDE the old García house. It was late afternoon, and dirt and dust and the smell of the house were in his clothes and in his hair and on his skin. At the far end of the south wall was a large pile of trash that he had hauled out of the three rooms. The steel-framed bed, the oak table, the rusted out woodstove, boards from the shelving, glass and empty cans and flat sheets of linoleum and, just off to the side of all that, a high mound of plaster slabs and dirt.

It hadn't taken him as long as he'd thought to clean the place out. He'd started at the south end of the house and worked his way through it, hauling everything outside, the bandana, stained black at the mouth, wrapped around his face. He'd finished all that around noon, eaten lunch, and then started tearing the loose plaster off the walls. All that was left inside was the cookstove and the crosses. The cookstove because it was too heavy to move, and the crosses because Will wasn't sure just what to do with them.

He was smoking a cigarette now, the smoke a little harsh in his throat after breathing so much dust, and looking out over the valley. Just down the hill was Manuela's house and beyond that was a large alfalfa field. The plants were stunted and yellowed from lack of water and the weeds and clover growing along the ditch that bordered it weren't much better. It had been a long, dry summer, and Will knew that whoever owned the field would have been lucky to get even one cutting.

Between Manuela's house and the field was a dirt road that ran by one field after another, past old, broken down corrals and abandoned adobes and trashed out trailers and towering cottonwoods until it finally swung back around to the highway. From where he stood, Will could see all the way across the valley to the low-lying hills far off to the west.

He thought about what he'd found in the wall and, whether it was the cigarette smoke that had calmed him or the sun shining warm or the sight of the village sitting quiet and still, it struck him that he must have made a mistake, that he'd been in the old house so long that his eyes and his mind had seen something that wasn't there, something that couldn't possibly be there. And even if he was wrong about that, it was far too late in the day to do anything about it now.

He glanced over his shoulder and thought that he ought to shut the place up before he left, but then he figured it might be better to leave all the doors and windows open. The place could air out overnight and besides, other than his tools, there was nothing in there to take. He took a last hit off his cigarette, dropped it to the ground, and stepped it out. Then he took the path back down the hill.

The front door to Manuela's house was cracked open. There wasn't a sound coming from inside. Will could smell the faint odor of coffee mixed with the stale scent of old clothes and old bedding and old age. A couple of wasps were flying slow and heavy at the upper edge of the doorframe. He watched as they lit on the frame and burrowed into a narrow crack between the mud and the wood. He stood there for a moment longer and then pulled the door all the way open and called out Manuela's name.

"I'm here, hijo," came her voice. "In the kitchen."

Will stepped inside. The room was small with a couple of closed doors off to the left that he figured must lead to bedrooms. An armchair was placed in front of the window with a small table beside it. A single bed was pushed up against the far wall. The mattress was covered by a quilt that was pulled up tight over a pillow. The floor was thick wood planks tightly fitted and the ceiling was low, the mud between the vigas painted white. A bare lightbulb hung from the ceiling and a lamp stood beside the armchair.

The first time he'd been here, he hadn't taken much notice of the place. But now it struck him that there was not one thing hanging on the walls, no pictures of saints or photographs of family or even a calendar from some lumberyard. There wasn't even a book or a magazine lying on the table or on the bed. He could have been standing in anybody's house anywhere, and he wondered why a woman as old as Manuela García would have so little of her life around her.

What does she do in this house? he wondered. He looked at one of the closed doors. Maybe she keeps her things in there, he thought. The things she cares about. Then, thinking what did it matter anyway, he crossed the room and went into the kitchen.

Manuela was at the sink. A slow run of water was flowing from the faucet. On the counter beside her was a bowl of crabapples. She was wearing the nightgown she'd had on that morning, and Will wondered if she'd had it on all day. It hung so low on her shoulders that he could see the ridges of her spine and the sharp line of her collar bone. Her hair was tied back behind her neck.

"I'm almost done here," Manuela said, without turning. "You did so much work up there today. I'm so proud of you."

She shut off the water. "Just let me finish, and then we can talk a little. I made some coffee for you."

Out the window in front, Will could see the old house. It seemed closer than it was, as if it had crept a few yards down the hill. He could see the pile of trash at one end, the sway to the roofline, and the dark holes where he'd left the windows open. He wondered if Manuela had watched him walk to her house.

"No," he said. "I can't stay. I just stopped to tell you I was leaving."

"Thank you for that, hijo," she said and turned her head. For a second, in the light, she seemed suddenly decades younger, her skin stretched smooth and tight, her eyes dark and clear. "You'll be back tomorrow?" she asked.

"Yes," Will said.

"So, how did things go in my grandfather's house?"

It took him a few seconds to answer. "Not too bad," he said, finally. "I've got most of it cleaned out."

"I can see that," she said. "I knew it wouldn't take you so long."

"There's one thing I wanted to tell you," he said, looking at her. "In the kitchen, in the far north room, I found crosses hanging on the wall. I wasn't sure what to do with them, so I left them there."

For a moment, she didn't speak but just stared at him. Then the muscles in her face relaxed and she said, "Take them out of there, hijo, and put them in that pile of garbage. I don't want them in that house. I don't want anything left in that house."

"Are you sure?"

"Yes, I'm sure."

"Did you know they were there?"

"No, hijo. I told you, I don't even remember when I was last in that house."

"There's not just a few of them," he said, giving it one more try. "There's got to be at least a hundred of them."

Manuela turned all the way around and reached for the small towel hanging from the stove. "I don't care how many there are. They don't mean anything to me." She dried her hands and smiled. "I'm glad it went so well today," she said. "My grandfather's house has waited a long time for you."

Will drove down the dirt road, away from Manuela García's house, past Bernabe Medina's place. The old man was outside, close to where he kept his sheep. Will had put his roof on some years before. It had been just after Bernabe's wife had died, and Will remembered that the old man had stayed inside the entire time, and when he'd paid him, his hand had shaken so badly that he'd had to write the check three times before he got it right. Will slowed down as he drove by and waved a hand, but Bernabe just stood staring, his arms at his sides.

Will followed the road until it swung wide and hit the highway. He hung a right and a mile later pulled into Tito's Bar. The lot in front was empty, and the only ones inside were Fred Sanchez and Nemecio Archuleta. They were drinking beer at each end of the bar.

The two of them had had a fight a few years before and hadn't spoken since. According to Rudy Duran, who had seen the whole thing, the two of them had been quietly arguing about whose fault it was that Mundo Segura had run his motorcycle into Paulo Espinosa's cow one night, Mundo's or Paulo's or the cow's. Nemecio, who'd thought he'd won this argument by blaming Mundo, was drinking from his beer when Felix, whose cousin was married to Mundo Segura's sister, suddenly grabbed one of the empty bottles off the bar and struck Nemecio on the side of the head. The blow, though startling, had been glancing and so weak that it hadn't even knocked Nemecio off his stool. And what had been funny was that after smacking Nemecio, Felix Sanchez went on drinking his beer as if what had just happened didn't have a thing to do with him.

"What happened next," Rudy told Will, shaking his head, "was almost a tragedy."

Rudy Duran told Will this story one day after work, and they'd both been on their second beer. "What kind of tragedy?" Will asked.

"The bad kind," Rudy said. "The kind you don't see coming," and he belched loudly.

Once Nemecio realized it was Felix who had hit him and not, as he'd first thought, something that had happened inside his own head, he picked up his own bottle that still had some beer in it and threw it as hard as he could at Felix. His throw was so poor that the bottle flew across the room and struck Delfino Vigil, who had just walked in the door to ask if anyone had seen his pigs that were lost somewhere in the village, in the middle of the forehead. After that, Rudy went on, the two borrachos flew at each other like a couple of old, sad roosters who had no claws and no beaks but only wings that could barely flap.

When Will asked what had happened next, Rudy had shrugged and said that the fight didn't last so long. That Tito, who was sick of the two of them, grabbed them both and threw them out into the parking lot. But the bad thing was that he had to step over Delfino, who thought he had been shot, to do this, and by accident he kicked Delfino in the mouth breaking his false teeth.

"I tell you," Rudy said, tossing his empty beer can off into an irrigation ditch. "You got to be careful out there."

Will stood in the doorway for a second, not sure if it was worth going inside or not. Then almost against his better judgment, he walked over to the bar and leaned against it. He kept a couple of stools between himself and Fred. "Where's Tito?" he asked.

"How should I know?" Fred said, lifting a hand, and then letting it fall. There were six empty bottles in front of him. Tito would leave them there so that he didn't have to bother with remembering how many Fred had drunk. At the other end of the bar, Nemecio drank from his own beer without looking over.

"It's not my job to know where everybody is," Fred went on. "I come here to drink my beer in peace, not answer people's stupid questions." He peered over at Will, his head low and nodding, his eyes blood red and damp. "If you want to know so bad, why don't you ask that little pendejo at the end of the bar where Tito is. He thinks he knows everything."

Will leaned forward a little and looked past Fred. "Hey, Nemecio," he said. "Where did Tito go?"

"He went to get his grandson," Nemecio said, his voice a little slurred, a little too loud. "He said to tell anyone who came in that he'd be back in a little while."

Will let out a long breath. He could feel his shirt filthy against his back, dirt and bits of straw digging into his skin. He wondered just how long it would take Tito to get back. All he wanted was a beer and a shower.

Fred reached over and pulled at the sleeve of Will's shirt. "How long you been here, anyway?" he said. "I remember when you first got here. Driving that old truck you had. You were lucky nobody ever shot you."

"Yeah," Will said, barely listening. "I guess I was."

Fred pulled at his sleeve again. "I hear you're working for that Manuela García," he said. "Maybe I could help you a little bit."

As far as Will knew, the last time Fred had worked was twelve, fifteen years ago for some guy from the west coast who built a house a few miles south of the village. Word was that it didn't work out so well for either of them.

"I don't know, Fred," Will said. "I'm just getting started, but I'll let you know if something comes up."

Fred pulled back his hand. "Sure you will," he said. "That's what you always say. Oh sí, you'll get back to me." He turned away and picked up his bottle and took a long drink. He put the beer down and belched softly. "I wouldn't work for her anyway," he said. "I wouldn't work for her even if you begged me to."

Will stared at him. He was unshaven, his skin dark and pitted. The knuckles on one hand were twisted and swollen. Will realized that for all the years he'd sort of known this man, he had no idea where he lived, and only saw him walking the highways to Tito's, or on a bar stool inside it. It made him feel a little sad, like he'd neglected some chained-up dog. But it didn't make him so sad that he'd ever consider even the thought of working with him.

"If you wouldn't work for her," Will said, "why'd you ask me?"

Fred turned his head and stared at Will. "Ask you what?" he said.

Will shook his head and smiled. He ran a hand through his hair. "I had a long, rotten day today, Fred," he said.

"You had a bad day today," Fred said, turning away. "You should have had my day if you want to know what a bad day is. My day was so bad that when I saw that pendejo Nemecio it almost made me happy." He peered over at the far end of the bar. "Yeah, you," he yelled. "I'm talking about you, you fucking pendejo."

"I'm not doing nothing," Nemecio said, staring straight ahead. "I'm not even listening to you."

Will glanced out the open door. He could see his truck

parked outside, and then saw a couple of the Fernandez boys, both underage, pull in in their father's old Cadillac. Two girls were in the back seat.

"Oh man," Will said, softly. He pushed off the bar and walked around it. He threw a couple of bills next to the cash register, grabbed a six-pack out of the cooler, nodded to Miguel Fernandez who was just strutting in, and got out of there, leaving the two old borrachos to themselves.

Estrella's pickup, an old, red International that her grandfather had left her when he died, was gone when Will pulled up to his house. He vaguely remembered her telling him before he'd left that morning that she and her sister, Monica, were going to visit their great grandmother and that she might be a little late.

Estrella and her sister had drunk too many wine coolers one night not so long ago and come upon the idea of writing a book about the history of their family. It will be a big book, Estrella had told Will later, because the story is so enormous. We will write about how our ancestors first came to this valley and the names of their families and how they helped to build the church and dig the irrigation ditches and the crops they grew and how they survived the long, hard winters years and years ago. All those things, she told her husband, we will write about. And, she went on, Monica and I have made a promise to each other that we will do this even if it takes years.

"How are you going to find out all this stuff?" Will had asked. They were in bed, which was where Estrella usually brought up things she thought important, almost, Will thought, as if she were aware there was no place for him to go and that he would have no choice but to listen. Usually, he didn't mind so much, but there were times when he was so tired that he didn't much care if his daughters were fighting too much or if they seemed too quiet or if Estrella had been rude to ignore Berna Gonzales or if the ants in the south wall would make it collapse on their daughter's heads, and if so, why didn't he do something about it. And if he dozed off in the middle of what his wife was saying, she was gracious enough not to wake him but would wait until the following evening to begin all over again.

"What do you mean find out?" Estrella said. She was lying on her back, staring up at the vigas. She let one hand stray over to Will's belly and moved her fingers lightly back and forth, thinking that this might keep him awake a while longer.

"I mean this village has been here a long time. How are you going to find out about things that happened two hundred years ago?" He reached down and took her hand. He brought it to his mouth and kissed it, and then brought it back down to his belly.

"We're going to ask Nana," Estrella said.

Carmela Rael was ninety-six years old. She had outlived her husband and all of her children until the only relatives she had left in the village were her two great granddaughters, Estrella and Monica, and their own children. The old woman lived alone in a small adobe not far from Monica, and at least once a day either she or Estrella would stop in to make sure Carmela had eaten or dressed herself and hadn't fallen or wandered over to the neighbors' to yell at them for something they had done fifty years ago, as she sometimes did.

She was a small, hunched-over old woman who spent her days moving things in her house from one place to another and sweeping at the red ants that lived beneath her portal. She spoke nearly entirely in Spanish, and the words that came from her mouth came out in short, rapid bursts, as if she had saved them up for a long time and was just waiting for the right moment to spit them out.

When Will was at Carmela Rael's house with his wife and her sister, the old woman would sometimes ignore him and only speak with her granddaughters, and often he knew she was talking about him. And when that happened, Monica would laugh at what she had said and Estrella would shake her head.

"Nana," she would say. "Stop this."

But there were other times when he would catch her staring at him, almost as if she knew something he didn't, and he would look back at her until she turned to one of her granddaughters and mumble something he didn't understand. But for all that, he kind of liked the old woman, even if he couldn't explain why.

"Well," Will said now to his wife. "She might get you back a hundred years. What about before then?"

Estrella turned her head toward him. She could just make out his features in the darkness. "You know how things are, Will," she said. "One story can lead to another, and there are so many old people in this village who remember so many things."

For a while, Will didn't speak. He just laid there thinking about what she had said. Finally, he said, "You're right. Who knows what you'll find when you begin." But what he thought was that there were so many things that people chose not to remember that she might never know what was true or not. He felt her hand move away from his and slide lower down his belly.

"I am so happy you are my husband," she said, and her voice was thick. "Do you know that?"

And he turned to her. "Yes," he said. "I know that."

When Will walked into the kitchen of his house, he found a note on the table.

> *Will,*
>
> *If you forgot, Monica and I are going to Nana's house. Lawrence said he would watch the girls.*

*We left later than I wanted and might not be
here when you get home. There is food on a
plate in the refrigerator.*

*Emilia asks that you please not eat her cupcake.
It's for school tomorrow.*

*We love you so much.*
*Estrella*

He had a feeling that he wasn't going to see his family for a
while. He could picture Estrella and Monica, each with a pen
and a pad of paper, in their grandmother's house. They'd be
sitting at the kitchen table making notes of everything the old
woman gleefully said. And even if she refused to tell them anything, he knew they'd end up back at Monica's drinking wine
coolers until one of them noticed how late it was.

After reading Estrella's note, Will stripped out of his clothes
and tossed them in a pile outside. Then he took a long, hot
shower and put on a clean pair of jeans and a long-sleeved shirt.
He didn't bother to heat up his dinner, but ate it cold. Then he
grabbed a beer and went outside.

By now, the light was fading and the air was dead still. The
juniper trees over by the creek were in full shadow. A mess of
small birds was flitting about noiselessly in the thick sagebrush
and dwarf piñon that grew just past the clearing around his
house. Although the sky was still lit with pale streaks of light,
the foothills off to the east lay soft and dark. From far off in the
distance, like a deep echo, came the low, hollow bawl of a cow.

Will lowered himself to the ground and leaned back against
the wall of his house. He could feel the heat trapped in the
adobe seeping warm through his shirt. He stretched out his
legs and crossed them at the ankles, his beer cradled in his lap.

Suddenly, a dull ache bit into his calf, like the muscle might cramp. He cursed and uncrossed his legs quickly and arched his foot until it eased. And then, slowly, he stretched them back out again.

There was a story he could almost remember. It was there in his head, but when he reached for it, like smoke it drifted away. He knew he had heard it a long time ago, but he couldn't remember where he'd heard it or who it had been about. Or even, for that matter, who had told it to him. Probably some old man, Will thought. One more story about this village told by some old man.

He took a drink from his beer and reached in his pocket for a cigarette. He lit it and blew out a slow stream of smoke. Then it came to him. He smiled a little.

"It was an old man," he breathed out. "It was Leonardo Martinez who told me the story."

He wasn't sure why Leonardo Martinez had suddenly come to mind. Maybe it had something to do with Fred Sanchez or Manuela García or the crosses hanging on the wall or what he thought he might have found in the wall of that old house. Or maybe it had nothing to do with anything but just some random memory that had surfaced for no reason.

He raised his beer and drank until the can was empty. Then he tossed it off to the side. Thirty years had passed since Will had heard Leonardo's story. The man had been dead for a long time now, and Will realized that he had heard the story even before he'd begun working with Felipe, and long before he had married Estrella.

He stubbed his cigarette out in the dirt and folded his hands in his lap. He closed his eyes and let his head drop until his chin rested on his chest. He could feel the chill in the air, and, like cold spots in water, it moved now and again over his face.

We were off by ourselves, he thought. Just the two of us. Somewhere out of the village. And then it all came rushing back, and he knew why Leonardo Martinez had come to mind. He remembered that he had heard the old man's story late one day not long after he had first come to Guadalupe. He had heard it on an empty stretch of land miles north of the village.

# THREE

❊ **ALTHOUGH WILL HAD SEEN** Leonardo Martinez now and again around the village, he hadn't taken much notice of him. After all, the place seemed to have more than its share of old men, and Leonardo was one more of them.

He was a small, scrawny old guy. He always wore the same grease-stained overalls that dragged a bit on the ground, a baseball cap pulled low, and thick-lensed glasses that made his eyes look bigger than they were. His upper teeth clicked in his mouth when he spoke, and he was missing a couple of fingers from his left hand. He was well into his seventies and walked with a slight limp, as if he'd hurt his leg not so long ago and the bones hadn't healed right. Will would see him at the lumberyard ordering parts from Joe Vigil, who ran the place, or catch sight of him driving his old, battered pickup slowly along the highway. The old man had a way of driving half on the pavement and half on the shoulder of the road. He'd be hunched over the steering wheel and peering out the far side window, as if there was something out there that he'd lost and was hoping to find.

Every so often, especially that first winter when the only work Will could find was thirty miles south in Las Sombras, he would stop at Felix's Cafe way before dawn for a coffee to drink on the ride.

The village would be dead still and quiet, a haze of wood smoke hanging over the valley. And while Will waited by the cash register, he would see the old man sitting by himself at the same table in front of the plate glass windows. He'd have his coat on, his legs pulled up, one hand in his lap, the other wrapped around a cup of coffee. There would be a cigarette smoldering in the ashtray. He'd be sitting there all alone, nodding absently at whoever came through the door and staring out at the empty highway and the village beyond. And every time Will noticed him, he would glance out the window, too, and all he would see was darkness and the shadow of the adobes across the highway.

Will didn't know much about him, only that he owned a backhoe and lived alone in a small house at the south end of the village. He scraped out a kind of living digging trenches and mixing mud for adobes and laying culverts across driveways and irrigation ditches. It was Joe Vigil who told Will that Leonardo might help him out.

"Go ask him," Joe had said. He was sitting behind a desk in his office, his hands behind his head, his legs stretched out. The surface of the desk was littered with receipts and catalogues and flat washers and shells for a .22 and screws and who knew what else. "Ask him and see what he says."

"You don't know anybody else?"

"No," Joe said, a little surprised that this gringo, who had suddenly appeared in the village like a lost dog, was pushing it. While it was true the man seemed to be smart enough to keep to himself and not bother people, it was also true that nobody wanted much to do with him. But what Joe found even more surprising was that he kind of liked him, even if he knew he wouldn't last long. After a while, he'd either get tired of not fitting in or someone would mess with him so bad that he'd leave. He remembered that last white guy who thought he'd liked it here. He'd been stupid enough to go into Tito's Bar one Friday night, and that was the last anybody ever saw of him. Joe swiveled in his chair a little.

"What's the problem with Leonardo?" he asked.

"There's no problem," Will said, not really wanting to put it into words. "I just think he's a little too banged up. Maybe a little too old."

"What do they do to old people where you come from," Joe said, "take them out in the woods and shoot them? He might be old, but he still has to eat. You're not going to make him dig the trench by hand, are you?"

"No," Will said.

"Are you going to pay him?"

"Yes."

Joe shook his head. "Damn," he said. "Are all you people like this, or is it just you?"

"Like what?"

"Like when you get an answer to a question you have to waste time talking about it."

For a second, Will didn't say anything. Then he smiled. He reached in his pocket for a cigarette and lit it. "No," he said. "We're not all like that. You just looked like you didn't have much to do today."

Joe grunted and let his feet drop to the floor. He pushed up in his chair. He thought that it was time for Will to leave, before he got pissed off or ended up drinking a beer with him.

"Let me know what happens," he said, shuffling some papers around, a couple of flat washers falling to the floor. "If he says no, maybe I can think of someone else. And let me give you some advice. If you're going to stay around here, maybe you should learn a little Spanish."

Will had caught up with Leonardo a few days later. He saw the old man's truck parked in front of Tito's Bar and swung off the highway and parked beside him. As Will was getting out of his pickup, Leonardo came limping out of the bar carrying a brown paper bag. When the old man got close, Will reached out and touched his arm.

"Mr. Martinez," he said. "Could I talk to you for a second?" And when the old man paused, Will went on to say that he'd gotten his name from Joe Vigil and wondered if he'd be interested in digging a foundation a few miles north of Guadalupe.

The old man squinted through his glasses and shifted the bottle from one arm to the other. He stared at Will for so long that Will wondered if he'd already forgotten what he'd asked and was trying to remember.

"I don't know you, do I?" he said, finally.

"No," Will said. "I haven't been here long."

"What kind of work did you say it was?"

"A foundation. A little north of here."

Just then, a vehicle pulled in next to Will's truck. A couple of guys got out. One of them gave Will a stare and then talked to Leonardo over the hood of his car. After a moment, he gave Will one more glance and went inside the bar. The old man shifted his bottle yet again and looked back at Will.

"I guess I got nothing to do tomorrow," he said. "Maybe we could take a look then."

The next day they met at the lumberyard and drove out of the village. Will led the way with Leonardo trailing behind, and as always the old man drove slow, his pickup half on the pavement and half off of it.

They drove north for ten miles and then turned east onto a road that was arroyoed out and not much more than ruts and loose dirt and rock. It wound through sparse, pale grass and scattered sage, and then climbed high onto a slope thick with piñon and juniper trees that rose all the way to the base of the foothills. Far below and to the east, the valley, flat and scarred deep where the river ran, stretched forever.

Will stopped at the edge of a small clearing overgrown with scrub oak and waited for Leonardo to catch up. He could hear the old man's truck down the hill, the engine straining, a cloud of gray exhaust just above the treeline. When he finally pulled up and stopped, Will walked over to where Leonardo sat in his pickup. The window was down and he was smiling a little.

"My truck hasn't worked this hard for a long time," Leonardo said, a slight whistling sound coming from his mouth.

"It's a ways up here, isn't it?" Will said. Even from a few feet away, he could feel waves of heat coming from the engine. There was a burning stench that he knew was the clutch.

"Oh, sí," Leonardo said. "It's pretty far up here all right."

"Well," Will said, half turning. "This is where the house goes."

"I see," Leonardo said, nodding his head.

The sun was shining through the windshield, glinting off the frame of the old man's glasses. Leonardo reached up and pulled down the visor and then put his hands back on the steering wheel. They were thin and boney, as if the moisture had been sucked out of them, and marked with old scabs. The two fingers that were missing on his left hand were stubbed below the first knuckle. He had a cigarette going and smoke drifted out the open window.

"I've got to clear out the scrub oak," Will said. "And maybe take down a few trees. But it's not going to be all that big. Somewhere around twenty by thirty feet."

"I see," Leonardo said, again. He looked around and shook his head. "Eee," he breathed out. "I forget how much rock is up here. But sometimes that's a good thing. You don't need to dig so deep. I think," and he rubbed the side of his face, "six to twelve inches should be plenty. There's no sense in digging up a bunch of rock and then throwing a bunch more back in the hole."

"Well," Will said, and the word dragged out a little bit. "I guess that's true. You should know what you're doing," although he was beginning to wonder. Where he came from foundations were two feet wide and three feet deep. He'd noticed that a lot of the adobes in Guadalupe had been built on nothing more than loose stone. He'd also noticed that every one of them had moved some, the roofs sagging, the walls leaning, as if they were tired and wanted to lie down.

"Oh sí," the old man said. "I know what I'm doing, all right. I've been working a backhoe for a long time now." He leaned forward, stubbed the butt of his cigarette in the ashtray, and sat back.

"I see what you need, my friend," he said. "But I don't think I can help you."

Will shook his head slightly and looked down at the ground. He wondered what Joe Vigil had been thinking, and then realized that it wasn't all Joe's fault, that he'd had a feeling from the beginning that Leonardo wasn't right for this job. It was too far away from Guadalupe, and even if Leonardo wasn't too old, he was too old to care about some things. He thought they could talk for a little while longer and then head back to the village. And later he could start all over again and come back up here with someone else.

He raised his head and looked back at the old man. "Maybe that's for the best," he said. "The road is pretty bad, and I wouldn't want you to wreck your truck."

"The road's pretty bad, all right," Leonardo said, nodding his head again. "But if you get a man who knows what he's doing, he could fix it fast. He could fill in some of those ruts and dig up some of those big rocks. It wouldn't take so long and it would be good as new." There were knots of dried saliva at both corners of his mouth. Behind his glasses, the edge of one eye was streaked wet.

"You'll find somebody else to do this," Leonardo went on. "Maybe one of those Tafoya brothers. They don't live so far away. Just don't get that Juan. He has a bad way about him, especially when he's not drinking. When he's drinking, he's okay to be around."

"All right," Will said, thinking this would be something to remember in case Joe mentioned Juan's name. "I'll remember that."

"His brother, Jose. You get him. He won't cheat you, and he's good with his machine." He looked past Will.

The scrub oak in the clearing was newly leafed out, the leaves so green they shimmered in the light. There were still some damp patches in the shade from where snow had melted not so long ago. Above, the sky was a pure blue, clouds beginning to build up over the mountains. All around was an endless stretch of trees that rose and fell with the lay of the land.

"I'm glad I came up here," Leonardo said. "I haven't seen this country for a long time." He raised his hand and pointed out the window. "See up there? My father used to hunt that canyon. Just a little ways past the first bend is a big meadow." He shook his head. "That's where Antonio Pacheco shot at an elk and hit his cousin, Claudio, in the foot. I think it was Antonio who shot him, but it might have been his brother, Aferino. I don't remember for sure. I always get them mixed up. But I do remember Claudio saying later that one minute he had two good feet and everything in his life was as it should be, and the next one of them was gone and things weren't so good anymore."

Leonardo dropped his arm and let it rest along the outside of the door. His tongue was messing with his upper teeth, moving them a little up and down. "That was a long time ago," he went on. "Back then, there were deer and elk all over these hills. And now there's not one track." He reached up and scratched at his chin. "I wonder where they all went."

"Maybe they were hunted out," Will said.

"Maybe," Leonardo said. "Or maybe they just left. Maybe they got tired of it here and went somewhere else to live."

A sudden gust of wind picked up out of nowhere, rushing up the hill through the piñon and sweeping into the clearing. Will ducked his head as the wind pushed against the pickup. He could hear the scrub oak being whipped about. And then, just like that, it was gone. When he raised his head, he saw Leonardo staring at him.

"Let me tell you something," the old man said. "Even if you get Jose Tafoya to help you out, I don't think you should do this job. I don't know who wants you to build this house, but they'll never live way up here. This hillside is too lonely. I think if a person wasn't careful, they could get lost in these woods."

Will opened his mouth to speak, and then closed it. The hillside had felt fine to him. At least it had until now. Now, as if Leonardo had conjured something up, it seemed a little too quiet, a little too empty, a little too far away. But, he thought, that might be what happens when you spend too much time with an old man whose life is pretty much behind him and about all he can do with the time left is to tell old stories that he isn't even sure are true.

Leonardo was probably right about one thing, though. No one would ever live up here for very long. It was just some dream someone had to get far away from everything and start all over again. But after a while, the place would end up like those old, abandoned adobes in Guadalupe. The doors and windows boarded up, the weeds grown high, a sad, empty feel to the place. Will looked back at the old man.

"I'll think about it," he said.

"Bueno," the old man said, slapping the steering wheel gently with the flat of his hand. "You do that. You seem like a good boy to me. I wouldn't want anything bad to happen to you." He pushed back his cap. His forehead was bone white and marked with brown spots. His eyes were blinking behind his glasses.

"I never seen you before," he said. "Where are you from, anyway?"

"Me?" Will said, and he jerked his head back slightly. It took him a few seconds to answer. "I was raised back East," he said, finally. "My father farmed, but he wasn't so good at it. It's all gone now."

Will had grown up in a flat, gray part of the country where the horizon was broken with clumps of dusty trees and sagging power lines and a few two-storied, dilapidated farmhouses that were much like his own. It was a place where nothing seemed to change much except maybe the weather. The winters would get so cold that the ground froze three feet deep, and if the cows weren't kept in, they'd freeze to death leaning against fence lines. And the summers seemed to be always too wet or too dry, and if the crops didn't rot from black mold, they grew stunted and yellowed from lack of water.

Will remembered the drawn, haggard look that never left his father's face. The empty barn that reeked of old hay and manure, and the flutter of birds up in the rafters. And even though he'd been gone from that place for a few years, he was surprised at how fast it all came rushing back.

"It's different there," Will said. "Like it got used up and nobody noticed."

"I'd like to see it someday," Leonardo said. "I've never left this valley." He reached up and rubbed at the side of his face. "I went to La Prada a couple of times for potatoes. That's pretty far away."

La Prada was across the valley, some fifty miles away. "That's a drive," Will said.

"Oh sí," Leonard said. "It took me a whole day to get there and back. And what's worse is the last bag I got the eyes were all growing sprouts and weren't good for one damn thing except putting them back in the ground."

"Well," Will said, thinking that they'd talked long enough. "That's too bad. La Prada's a long way to go for nothing." He glanced down the hill. "Maybe we ought to get out of here now."

"What about the rest of your family?" the old man said. "Where are they?"

The sun was beginning to sink, and Will could feel a chill starting to set in. Far up the hill, he watched a small flock of ravens settle into the high branches of a ponderosa pine.

"I don't have any family left," he said. "They're either dead or gone." He slapped the driver's door with the back of his hand. "I'm going to head back down the hill, Mr. Martinez. I'll see you back in Guadalupe." Then he turned and took a step away.

"I was born a twin," Leonardo said, his voice a little louder. "Did you know that?"

Will stopped and looked back and stared at the old man for a few seconds. "No," he finally said. "I didn't know that." He couldn't imagine there being two of this old man.

"It's true," Leonardo said. His hand was still hanging down the outside of the pickup. It was trembling a little, his finger-nails tapping against the metal. He was gazing past Will. "He was named Benito. We weren't the kind of twins that look alike. We were the other kind. The kind that don't look the same but are still twins. You know what I mean?"

"Yes," Will said. "I know what you mean. So, where is your brother now?"

"Where is he?" Leonardo said. "He's gone. He got lost a long time ago."

"He got lost?" Will said and half smiled. He wasn't exactly sure what the old man meant. There wasn't all that much to Guadalupe. The valley stretched just a few miles north and south, and about a mile and a half wide. Will couldn't imagine how anyone could get lost in a place so small.

"You mean he left," he said.

The old man moved his eyes back to Will. "No," he said. "That's not what I mean. I mean my brother got lost when we were little. It's a long story. I can tell you, if you like."

The hillside was dead still, not a thing moving. The sun had fallen even lower. There was a sharp, thin feel to the light. Will took a step back toward Leonardo.

"All right," he said. "I guess there's nothing I need to get back for. Tell me. Tell me the story."

"My brother's name was Benito," Leonardo said, "and our mother told us that he didn't want to be born." He was smoking now inside the truck, little puffs of smoke wafting out the open window.

"She said that Benito stayed inside her for a long time after I was born, like he was hiding and thought that if he kept quiet no one would notice him. She said that when he finally decided to come out, he came so fast that the midwife, who was thinking about nothing but drinking a cup of sweet coffee with whiskey, threw up her hands and screamed. She was an old, old woman, one of those Garcías. Later, when my mother asked why she had been so frightened, the midwife said that she had never seen twins before, and was afraid that every baby she'd brought into this world was suddenly going to appear, and that there were a few she didn't want to see." Leonardo shook his head and smiled.

"Let me tell you something," he said. "The first sound a new baby should hear should not be the sound of some old García woman screaming. I think this life is hard enough without hearing that, don't you?"

"Yes," Will said, beginning to wonder about just what kind of story he was being told. "I think you're right. I think this life is hard enough."

Leonardo grunted and waved a hand. "But those Garcías," he said, "you've got to watch out for them. I remember when Esperanza García threw a big rock at a dog and hit the priest in the back of the head by mistake. At least, she said it was a mistake. There was some trouble about that, especially when the priest began to forget things. He'd forget to light the candles by the altar, and forget to wear his robes, and sometimes forget what day to say Mass. And when he didn't, his sermons were full of strange things that no one would dream Jesus would ever think of doing. It got so bad that he even forgot he was a priest and started messing with Pablo Ruiz's wife. And worse, not long after that, he left the village altogether with Paco Sandoval's oldest boy and neither one of them was ever seen again." Leonardo stopped talking and stared hard at Will.

"If you're going to stay around here," he said, "keep away from those Garcías. They're nothing but trouble."

"I'll remember that," Will said. The only García he knew drove a truck for the lumberyard. As far as he could tell, the guy seemed okay. He thought it might be best to keep Leonardo's opinions to himself. He had enough problems in Guadalupe as it was.

For a little while, neither of them spoke. Leonardo's cigarette had burned out, and he was staring out the windshield at the growing shadows. The ravens, with a piercing cry, rose out of the ponderosa tree. They circled for a moment, and then swooped low over the clearing, their wings beating air, and flew off down the hill.

"What about your brother?" Will said.

"I know," Leonardo said. "I know. I didn't forget. I was remembering." He took in a sharp breath and let it out slowly. "Do you know what our mother would tell the two of us over and over again?" he asked.

"No," Will said. "I don't."

"She would tell Benito that of all the things in her life he was her greatest gift, that he was born when no one would ever have thought to look for him. Then she'd turn and look at me. And you, Leonardo, she'd say. You are my first born, and since you are so much older than your brother, you must always, always look out for him." Leonardo turned his head and looked at Will.

"I don't know what happened," the old man said. "I only know that I didn't do so good at what my mother asked." He moved his hand to his shirt pocket, and then let it drop to his lap.

"My brother was lost one warm summer night that was no different from any other," he said. "And to this day, I don't know how such a thing could have happened."

That evening, as usual, Leonardo and Benito's mother was washing the dishes and gazing out the window over the sink at the apricot trees by the ditch. She reminded herself that tomorrow she would have her sons gather up the rotten fruit before her yard became a place for bees and skunks and even the bears that would sometimes wander out of the hills looking for food. The last thing she needed, she thought, was for one of her sons to be sprayed by a skunk or stung by bees. And if that were to happen, and she smiled a little, she knew it would be Benito who would be sprayed or stung while Leonardo stood safely out of danger, staring wide-eyed at what he would think was his fault. She closed her eyes, her hands moving slowly in the warm water.

"Mi hijos," she said, softly.

At the same moment their mother was imagining Benito swarmed with bees, their father was outside fixing the fence his pigs had once again managed to knock down. The last time they had gotten loose, they had chased Jose Archuleta's cows until, in a frenzy, they broke through their own fence and disappeared into the low-lying hills west of the village.

"You're a good neighbor," Jose had said when he came to the Martinez house to complain. "But I don't know about those pigs of yours. They don't act like pigs, they act like mean dogs. So you warn them for me that if I ever see them in my fields again, I'll set my own dogs on them, and then I'll shoot them, and then I won't even eat them. I'll hang them from my fence so every pig in this village knows what will happen to them if they chase cows."

Leonardo and Benito had been helping their father set the cedar posts until finally, in disgust, he shook his head and told them that they'd helped him more than enough, that they could go off and do what they wanted for a little while before bed. Then he straightened up and stared hard at them.

"Don't either of you forget about Juanito," he said. "I don't want to catch you anywhere near the ditch."

The ditches that summer were running full, and just a week before, Juanito Griego had fallen in and drowned while playing with his sister, Victoria.

"Papa," Leonardo said. "Is it true Victoria pushed Juanito into the water?"

For a moment, their father didn't say a word. Then he shook his head and said, "Where did you hear such a thing?"

"Benito told me," Leonardo said.

"I didn't tell you that," Benito said, quickly. "I told you maybe she pushed him."

"No, you didn't," Leonardo said. "You said that when Juanito wasn't looking, she gave him a push."

"Well, she's always pushing at school. She pushed Lito so hard he fell over and hit his head on the stove. And look what she did to Octaviano. He was just standing there doing nothing when she hit him with a stick."

"That doesn't mean she pushed Juanito."

"Eee, can you two be quiet?" their father said, his voice raised. He crouched down before his two sons. "I don't know how Juanito fell into the ditch, but I never want to hear either of you talk this way again. Victoria feels bad enough without you two telling stories about her. Do you understand?"

"Yes," the two boys said.

"Now go," their father said, standing up. "Before I change my mind. And don't forget what I said about the ditch."

Leonardo and Benito ran as fast as they could along the edge of the alfalfa field and out to the road. They stopped to catch their breath where the path to the creek met the road.

"Let's go see the fish, Leonardo," Benito said. Earlier that day, the two of them had thrown a thousand rocks in the creek so that the water would pool. It had been Benito's idea that the fish would swim in and get stuck, and then he and Leonardo could hit them with sticks.

Leonardo glanced down the path that led through a maze of piñon and juniper trees. Although it wasn't quite dark, it was dark enough for Leonardo to know that the last place he wanted to be was on a narrow path surrounded by trees and shadows. He looked back over his shoulder and saw that their mother had lit the lamps in the house.

"It's too late," he said. "And papa said not to go there."

"Papa said not to go to the ditch," Benito said. "He didn't say nothing about the creek." He came up close to his brother and put his hands on his shoulders. The two of them were almost the same height. Benito was a little taller, his face a little thinner. He rested his forehead against Leonardo's.

"Let's go, Leonardo," he said, and Leonardo could feel his brother's breath warm on his face. "I'll go first and you can follow me."

"It's too dark to see the fish, Benito," the boy said.

"We don't need to see them. We'll hear them flopping." He pictured the look on his father's face when they walked into the house with a hundred fish.

"What if the dog got loose again?" Leonardo said.

A month or so before, Benito had been running down the road when the Archuleta dog had sprung out of nowhere, not only knocking Benito down, but running off with one of his shoes.

"You must always be careful," their mother had told the two of them later. "At any moment something might happen. You should stay with your brother, Benito, and not go running off. You were lucky today that all the dog wanted was your shoe." Then she had leaned back in her chair and shook her head.

"For someone who was so slow to be born," she had said, "I don't know why you are always in such a hurry." And maybe the greatest difference between the two brothers was that Leonardo would never forget what their mother had said, and Benito already had.

"Eee," Benito breathed out. "That happened just that one time. Besides, the Archuletas keep him chained up at night."

"How do you know that?" Leonardo said, knowing full well that his brother was only saying what he wanted to believe. From far down the road, he heard the sharp voice of the old García woman yelling at her son, who was himself an old man, to come inside and help her to bed. Every so often, there came the dull sound of their father's sledge hammer as it struck the flat end of a cedar post.

"I just know, Leonardo," Benito said, and he pulled back a little. "Nothing bad will happen. I promise you. We'll go fast

fast and come right back." And then he gave his brother a little push and turned and ran off down the path, his arms flapping.

"Venga, Leonardo," he called out, without looking back. "I'll race you."

For a moment, the boy stood on the road, staring at where his brother had gone. And then he began to follow slowly. He walked looking down at the ground, keeping his eyes away from the shadows around him. He could hear the whine of mosquitoes and the noise of crickets. And whenever a branch grabbed at his shirt, he would jerk his arm back and hold it tight against his body. From deeper in the woods came the sound of a mourning dove.

When he finally came to where the end of the path met the creek, Benito was nowhere to be seen. It was too dark now to see the water, let alone what fish might be in it.

"Benito," Leonardo called out, softly. He was close to tears and didn't know why. "Where are you, Benito?" He's hiding, the boy thought, and at any moment he'll jump out at me.

"Benito," he said again, louder. "I don't want you to scare me." But there was no answer, and all there was to hear was the soft sound of water running and a stir of branches.

"What happened to him?" Will asked, thinking that this couldn't be the end of Leonardo's story, that no story ended this way.

The old man had fallen quiet. Somewhere along the way, he had lit another cigarette and was sitting inside the cab smoking it quietly. His story had gone on for a long time, and now it was close to dark, the air cool and still.

"What happened to him?" Leonardo said, blowing out a slow stream of smoke. "I don't know what happened to my brother." He turned his face to Will. "I stayed there for a little while calling him, and then I ran home, hoping he was there.

45

When I walked into my house, my mother took one look and asked where Benito was. I told her that he had gone to the creek, and then she went outside and called for him. When there was no answer, she sent my father, who was still with the pigs, to look for him. My mother and I stayed behind."

The old man took one last hit off his cigarette and let it drop outside the window. "Don't worry, hijo, my mother told me. Your father will find him. You'll see, soon they both will come walking through the door." The old man grunted softly. "That's not what happened."

Will wasn't sure what to say. He and Leonardo had spent a long time wandering through the old man's mind but, at the end, something important had been left unsaid, something Leonardo had failed to mention, or maybe something he hadn't understood or hadn't been told way back then. Again, he thought that no one could disappear in a place as small as Guadalupe.

"What about the creek?" he asked.

"No," the old man said. "The creek was running low. All the water was going to the ditches."

"Somebody must have seen something," Will said.

"I don't know about that," Leonardo said, shrugging his shoulders. "All I know is that people looked for him everywhere. They searched for him all night and for days after. They looked along the creek and in old, abandoned houses and even far up into the foothills, thinking that maybe he'd run away for a reason no one knew, or that some animal had carried him off. My mother and father asked me over and over again what had happened, but there wasn't one thing I could tell them that I hadn't already said. One minute my brother was here, and the next, as if the village had swallowed him up, he was gone."

Leonardo let out a long breath, and moved his eyes back to Will. Then he smiled a little. "I don't tell people this," he said, his voice so low that Will had to lean forward to hear, "but I still look for him. When I'm drinking coffee in the cafe or driving the roads, I always keep my eyes open for Benito. And there are some times when I think maybe I see him running across a field or walking through the trees along the ditch or way far ahead of me in the weeds along the side of the highway. And you know what I say to myself? I say, there you are, Benito, you couldn't hide from me forever. Finally, I've found you. But what's funny is that I'm an old man now, and he's still a little boy." He grunted and shook his head.

"I don't know how that can be," he said. "Do you?"

"No," Will said. It was so dark now that he could barely make out the old man's face. "I don't know how that could be."

Leonardo grunted again, and then, his hands on the steering wheel, pulled himself up a little. "Life is funny," he said. Then he cocked his head sideways and glanced at Will. "Hey," he said, his voice a little excited this time. "Did I tell you that Benito was my twin brother?"

It was dark now. Will could feel cold seeping through the back of his shirt, could feel it lying on his bare arms. He raised his head and shook it a little. He felt as if he might have dozed off, as if the memory of Leonardo's story had been half real and half a dream.

"It was a long time ago," he muttered. "We took that drive a long time ago."

He leaned his head back against the wall. A million stars were in the sky, and a sliver of moon hung just above the foothills.

From the creek came the sound of some small animal moving through the brush. He glanced over at the long drive that led to his house and wondered what his wife was doing, if his daughters were asleep on their tía's bed or if they were still running with their cousins. And then, as he sat leaning back against the adobe wall, he remembered what Leonardo's mother had told her son what now had to be more than a hundred years ago.

"You must always be careful, mi hijos," she had told them. "At any moment something might happen."

# FOUR

&#9774;WILL WAS STILL ASLEEP when Estrella woke up the next morning. One of her legs was thrown across his and the other was half on the bed and half off, her bare foot chilled. She dragged it back beneath the blankets and looked over at her husband. He was sleeping with his face buried in the pillow, his breath a little ragged, as if he was slowly suffocating or a bad dream was going in his mind. She said his name softly until he moaned a little and shifted his head. A second later, his breathing calmed. There, she thought.

Although it was still dark out, she could feel that dawn was not far off. Outside the window, the darkness seemed to be a shade lighter, and there was the far-off sound of the small birds that lived in the trees by the creek. Other than the occasional creak of a floorboard or the settling of a viga overhead, the house was still. She'd gotten home late the night before and knew that her daughters would sleep until the moment she woke them for school.

She slid up a little higher on the bed, careful not to wake Will, and rested her head back against the wall. I'll just lie here for a little while, she thought, and then the evening before crept into her mind, and she moaned softly. She closed her eyes and shook her head. "I don't believe what I heard," she whispered.

"Why do you care about all that?" Nana had asked her granddaughters. She was sitting beside Monica at the kitchen table. Estrella was across from the two of them, a pen in her hand, a lined notebook open before her. A bug was crawling across the plastic tablecloth, and Estrella watched as her grandmother's hand darted out and pinched it hard between two fingers. Then she dropped it to the floor and placed her hand back in her lap.

"I don't know why you care about things that happened so long ago," she said.

The old woman was so hunched over that it seemed as though she was speaking to the floor. She reminded Estrella of one of her daughters who had been scolded and was now part angry and part sulking at having to explain herself.

"We just want to know what you remember," Monica said, touching her grandmother's shoulder. "So that none of it is ever forgotten."

"Some things should be forgotten," the old woman said. Her jaw was moving, as if chewing, and a thin thread of saliva hung from her mouth to her lap. Monica wiped at it with her sleeve.

"Tell us what the village was like when you were a girl," Monica said, hoping this would get her going a little.

For a moment, the old woman just sat there, her head trembling, her mouth still moving. Finally, she said, "What do you think it was like? It was smaller back then, and there was more rain. But things are always smaller when it rains."

Estrella glanced down at her notebook. She wondered if this was something she should write down. She thought that even if she had no idea what her grandmother meant, maybe later it would become clear.

"You're going to write that down?" Monica said.

Estrella looked at her sister. "Maybe it's important," she said.

"What, that the village shrinks when it rains and gets bigger when it doesn't? If we write everything down, the book will be filled with recipes and plumbing problems."

"Maybe you're asking the wrong questions," Estrella said. Their plan had been for Monica, who was four years older and her grandmother's favorite, to ask the questions and for Estrella to write down what she said.

"What questions do you think I should ask?" Monica said.

"Maybe about our grandfather or her children or who her neighbors were back then."

Seeing the serious expression on her sister's face suddenly made Monica want to laugh out loud. She knew if that was to happen, Nana would get up from the table and, without a word to either of them, go to her bedroom and lie down. She bit down hard on her lip and looked at her grandmother. "What about our grandfather?" she asked. "How old were you when the two of you met?"

"I'll tell you something you don't know," the old woman said, the words rushing out of her mouth.

Monica reached over and smoothed the old woman's hair. "What don't we know, Nana?" she asked.

"I'll bet you don't know you're a Jew, do you?" Nana said. "I bet you didn't know that. Not even the priest knew that. In Spain, it was the priests who cut all the Jews up into little pieces. The priests were the last people we'd tell." Her head was shaking more now, and she twisted her neck and looked up at Monica, who was staring back at her, her mouth open.

"Oh sí, you're a Jew all right," the old woman went on. "The first Rael to come to this valley was Solomon Rael, and he was one big Jew, and so was his wife and twelve children. Jews, all of them." The old woman turned her head and looked down at the table top. She could see a deep burn in the wood from when her husband had let his cigarette lie there until it turned to ash. She put a finger in the scar and moved it back and forth. He had been dead a long time.

"Grandmother," Monica said, and there was a nervous smile on her face. "We've been baptized and confirmed. I've been married in the church."

"So?" Nana said. "Jews get married, too, don't you know."

Monica shook her head. "That's not what I mean. I mean if that was true, how could we not have known?"

The old woman put her hand in her lap, and looked again at her favorite granddaughter. "There are a lot of things you don't know," she said.

Monica stared back at her grandmother. Then she said, "Like what?"

"Did you know that your great great great great grandfather was named Mercolino Rael? He was a weak man who couldn't even tell his wife, who was his first cousin and was known to always speak her mind even if what she spoke was wrong, which was always, to be quiet. His children were nasty little things, and his cows bit him whenever he came close. It was his wife, a Rael también, who made him go to the church one day in the rain to help hang a young boy from the cottonwood tree for something he didn't do. And there was your great great Tío Alfredo who would take a wagon down south and buy or steal young Indian girls. And you can guess what he did with them. And your great Tía Lucia who slept with every Medina in the village and still called her sons Raels. Oh sí, I know some things." She looked at Estrella, who, like her sister, just sat there staring.

"You should write all of these things down, Estrella," the old woman said, waving a hand. "Write down that you are a Jew and that your grandfather hung a poor boy at the church."

And here, she paused for a moment, as if to catch her breath. Her head had dipped even lower so that her chin was barely above the top of the table.

"Grandmother," Estrella said. She was close to crying and didn't know why.

The old woman shook her head. "And tell that husband of yours that he should be careful working for Manuela García. Tell him that there has always been something wrong about her. Tell him that she, too, has her secrets."

Later, at Monica's house, after quickly drinking two wine coolers, Monica told her sister that she wasn't sure if she wanted to write this book anymore. And when Estrella, who was still badly confused about what their grandmother had told them, asked why, Monica said that talking to Nana was like making things up, that they would never ever be sure what was true and what wasn't.

"You mean about our being Jewish?" Estrella said. "Or that we might be related to the Medinas?"

Monica smiled and reached across the table and took her sister's hand. The rest of the house was still. Ella and Emilia, along with their cousins, had fallen asleep on the living room floor. And Lawrence, after four beers, was asleep in his chair.

"Both," Monica said. "All of it. Everything that Nana said."

"Do you think it's a lie?"

"I don't know what I think. But I know I didn't think I was going to hear what I heard. And this after asking Nana only a few questions. Who knows what she'll tell us if we keep asking." She had thought that the book would be full of names and dates and the places their ancestors came from and what they did when they came to Guadalupe. It would be about their great Tío Federico who opened a feed store next to Felix's Cafe and his son, Francisco, who somehow accidently burned it down three times, and how a distant cousin once saw Kit Carson ride a mule through the village early one cold, winter morning. It would be about all of that, and even if there were a few odd things in the book, there would be a sweetness to all of it. It certainly wasn't going to be about how their Tía Lucia slept with every Medina and a grandfather who hung some poor boy at the church and how the entire Rael family was descended from Jews. And if that was true, not only had her ancestors fled from the church, but had then journeyed thousands of miles just to build another one that not one of them believed in.

She could feel a headache coming on and wished that her husband had had the graciousness to get their children into bed instead of leaving them asleep on the floor like dogs. She let go of Estrella's hand, leaned back in her chair, and took a long drink from her wine cooler.

"I don't know, Estrella," she said. "Maybe we should talk about this tomorrow."

"What do you think Nana meant about Manuela García?" Estrella asked.

"How should I know?" Monica said. She had almost forgotten that Manuela García's name had even come up. "It's probably nothing," she said. "You know how things are. More than likely one of their sons hit the other with a rock eighty years ago, and she still hasn't forgotten. What else could it be?"

The light outside the bedroom window was a shade lighter now, and Estrella knew she should get up. It would take some time just getting her daughters out of bed, and then there was breakfast and lunches to make and getting them out of the house so that they didn't miss the bus. She slid down lower on the bed and rolled against Will. She wrapped an arm around his belly and pulled herself even closer.

"Will," she said. "It's getting late."

"I know," Will said. "I'm awake." He'd been lying there for a while watching it grow light outside, putting off the moment he had to get out of bed.

"Are you going to work today?"

"Yes," he said, and rolled onto his back. Estrella lifted up a little, pulled his arm wide and then laid back down so that her head rested on his shoulder. She slung one leg over his. He could feel her breath warm on his skin. He moved his hand to the back of her head and threaded his fingers through her hair.

"I need to get up," he said after a while. Then he looked down at her. "You were late last night." He wasn't sure just what time Estrella had gotten home, but when he'd heard her drive up, he'd gotten out of bed and helped her carry the girls from the truck to their room. By the time Estrella had finally slid into bed, he was half asleep. And when she'd whispered his name, he hadn't answered, but turned away, hoping whatever she had to tell him could wait until morning.

"Nana told us that our family is Jewish, and full of murderers and adulterers, and even an uncle who kidnapped little girls. And I don't even want to know what he did to them. And that's just some of the things she told us."

For a moment, Will just laid there staring up at the ceiling, his fingers moving slowly through his wife's hair. He could picture the old woman, her head nodding, her back hunched, spitting out words about the Raels and then waiting to see the look on her granddaughter's faces. He grunted and shook his head.

"I think she likes doing this to you," he said.

"No," Estrella said, slapping his chest lightly. "Don't say that about her. My Nana's a sweetie."

Will thought that sweet might be the last word he'd use to describe Carmella Rael, that it might take a lot more than sweet to outlive nearly everyone in your entire family." Do you

55

remember last year when she told you that the owl in her apple tree was Rufino Trujillo?"

"Yes," Estrella said, and he could feel her smile against his skin.

"Do you remember that she wanted you to shoot it so it wouldn't bother her anymore?"

"Yes, I remember."

"Did you believe that?"

"Well," Estrella said, and she said the word slowly. "I didn't not believe it."

At the time, Estrella had thought it was a stretch to believe that Rufino Trujillo, who had died of old age just days before, had not only managed to turn himself into an owl, but had then chosen to roost in her grandmother's tree as if he still harbored some long-forgotten grudge. But on the other hand, she had a husband and two daughters whom she loved, and thought it best not to take any chances. What she told her grandmother was that since she would never have shot Rufino Trujillo when he was alive, she didn't feel it was right to shoot him now that he was dead. She told her grandmother that she shouldn't worry about this, that she would talk to Monica and the two of them would figure out what to do. By the time the two sisters had finally decided to let their husbands shoot the owl, Rufino had, thankfully, flown off and wasn't seen again in their grandmother's apple tree.

"But this isn't like that," Estrella said. "This is different. This seems bigger to me."

"What does Monica think?"

"She doesn't want to think about it. All she said was that she would appreciate it if I wouldn't tell Lawrence. You know how he is."

Lawrence was one of those guys who didn't think much about anything. He was good at filling in potholes for the county and mowing weeds along the side of the highway, but if he came to a crossroads, he'd sit there waiting for somebody to tell him which way to go. Will figured it wouldn't bother the man so much if his wife's ancestors were full of murderers and kidnappers and rapists, but that he might not be so happy about hearing that his family had become Jewish overnight.

Estrella propped herself up on one elbow and moved her hair back away from Will's face. "What do you think, Will?" she asked.

"I don't know," he said. "But I have a feeling if you looked hard enough you'd find something pretty bad in everybody's family."

Estrella grunted softly. " All we had to do was ask one question and suddenly one horrible story after another came out of Nana's mouth. She didn't have one good thing to say about anyone, Will."

"Look," he said. "Even if it's all true, what would it change?"

"How can you say that? What if you woke up one morning to find out that you were a Jew and your aunt slept with the whole village? How would that make you feel? I've spent my whole life praying to Jesus, and now I find out that everyone else in my family was just making believe."

She gazed out the open doorway that led to the rest of the house. Even though the light in the room was dim, Will could see how dark and smooth her skin was. Sometimes he thought she seemed too young to be with him, almost too young to be with anyone.

"Maybe it would change everything," Estrella said, slowly, still looking away. "It would mean that everything I thought was true about myself wouldn't be. It would mean my whole life was a lie."

Will shook his head and reached up and touched her face. "Don't get too carried away with this," he said. "Who knows what she'll tell you the next time you and Monica talk to her? Maybe she's saving up all the good stuff," although he had a feeling that whatever Estrella and Monica had tapped into, it was just the beginning.

Estrella grunted, and then she smiled. "Maybe," she said. "Maybe you're right. I'll tell that to Monica." She looked down at her husband. She could see how deep the lines were that ran from his eyes down his face and creased his forehead. She could see the gray in his hair and that he needed to shave. She bent down quickly and kissed him.

"Do you need to go right now?" she asked.

"Yes," Will said. "I'm already late."

"Do you know what Nana said about Manuela García?"

"No," Will said, and felt something shift inside of him.

"She said that Manuela García was wrong."

"Wrong about what?"

"Not that kind of wrong. The other kind. The kind where there is something wrong about her. She also said that she has her secrets, too."

He almost told her about what he thought he might have found in the wall of Manuela García's old house. But it went through his mind, especially feeling his wife's body warm against his, that there was a good chance he'd been mistaken. I'll tell her later, he thought. When I'm sure.

"Well," he said. "She's been all right so far." And then, as if from nowhere, the sight of Manuela García turning toward him, her nightgown slung low, her face stretched smooth, her eyes dark and clear, came rushing back to him. He shook his head a little.

"There's something about her, though," he said.

"Something what?"

"I can't quite put my finger on it," he told her. "It's like she changes. One minute she's this way and the next she's like someone else." He spit out a breath. "You know what she is? She's an old woman who's been alone for far too long. That's all."

For a few seconds, Estrella just stared down at him. And then she said. "You just be careful over there. I don't want some woman, even if she is old, messing with my husband." And then, in one motion, she threw the blankets off the two of them and jumped out of bed.

"Time to get up," she said, standing naked in front of the window, her hands on her hips. "Come on, you lazy, you can help me with the girls before you go."

By the time the girls were finally out of the house, the sun had risen above the mountains and the chill that had been in the morning air was gone. They'd missed the bus and were complaining about how tired they were as Estrella herded them out the door to her truck.

"Then you shouldn't sleep on the floor of your cousin's house," Estrella said. She squatted down and wiped something from Emilia's face with the sleeve of her shirt.

"There was no other place to sleep," Ella said.

"Your cousins have beds, don't they?" She stood up and looked at her oldest daughter. The girl was eleven years old and tall and lanky. Her face was round and her hair brown, like Will's, and long. Her skin was fair, not as dark as her younger sister's.

Ella shrugged her shoulders up and down. A backpack was slung around one arm, and in it were her books and her lunch and a sweater in case it got cold and a picture of her father as a boy that she carried everywhere with her. "Tío Lawrence didn't tell us to go to bed," she said.

"Tío Lawrence never tells anybody anything," Estrella said. "You should know that."

"He farts when he drinks beer," Emilia said, rubbing the place on her face that her mother had wiped clean. "He can make the floor shake with his farts."

Estrella pulled open the passenger door to her truck. "Get in," she said.

"I forgot my cupcake," Emilia said.

"Your cupcake is in your lunch," Estrella said. "Now get in the truck, we're late enough as it is."

"I think we should just stay home today," Ella said. "We don't do anything in school anyway."

Will was over by his truck, watching all this. He was usually gone when his daughters left for school, and he wondered if Estrella went through this every morning. Finally, shaking his head, he called out, "Hey, you two. Quit giving your mother a hard time and get in the truck."

"Can we take a walk when you get home from work?" Emilia asked.

"Yes," Will said. "We can take a walk, Emilia. But I'm not going to walk anywhere with you if you don't get in the truck."

He watched them climb into the old pickup, barely enough room for the three of them in the front seat. Estrella stretched out her arm and pulled her daughters back against the seat. Then she leaned over the steering wheel. She gave Will a smile, mouthed goodbye, and shoved the truck into gear. They hadn't gone thirty feet when Emilia stuck her arm straight out the side window, and he heard Estrella yell at her to get it back in the cab before something bad happened. He waited until they swung around the curve by the creek and disappeared into the trees and willows that grew there. Then he got into his own pickup and left.

When he got to where the end of his drive met the dirt road, he came to a stop. The road was shadowed here, rimmed by large cottonwood trees. He could feel a wash of cool air coming in the open window. Across the road from him was an empty field. A few years back, it had been lush and green with alfalfa. Now, it had gone to weed, and even those looked burnt and dried up. At the south end was an old ruin, not much more than eroded adobe bricks pitted with gun shots. A few old boards, gray and warped, were scattered about. Beyond that a couple of beat-up trailers were set back in the trees, old junked cars covered with leaves and dirt parked off to the side. Will sat there for a moment staring out the windshield.

"Well," he said out loud. And then, instead of turning in the direction of Manuela García's place, he hung a right. He thought that maybe it was time to go see Felipe.

# FIVE

✾WILL SAWYER AND FELIPE GRIEGO met more than thirty years ago on a jobsite in Las Sombras.

Although Felipe had seen Will driving around Guadalupe and heard about this gringo who had moved into the village like it was his own, he thought it best to keep his distance. After all, he'd been born and raised in Guadalupe and had more than enough friends and family as it was. He figured that even if it was okay to work with the guy, the last thing he needed was some jodido from somewhere else bothering him about where was the best place to cut wood or who in the village was related to who or whether they could drink a beer together at Tito's where Will would more than likely get the shit kicked out of him while Felipe stood there not knowing what to do.

What changed everything was Felipe's truck broke down and his wife, Elena, refused to let him take her small car.

"No," she'd said. "You cannot have my car. I have to take Isidro to the clinic and then I have to see my mother." Isidro was suffering from an earache that, no matter how much garlic Elena had put in his ear, had kept him up most of the night, and since today was Tuesday she would, as usual, go see her mother to drink coffee and talk about things.

"Why don't you call that man you're working with?" she went on. "You can ride with him until you get your truck fixed. I don't know why you drive all that way in two trucks, anyway. "

They rode back and forth to Las Sombras together for a couple of weeks, sharing coffee and gas. And when the job ended some time later, Felipe, in a rare good mood and against his better judgment, asked Will if he'd help him strip some shingles off his neighbor's roof and nail on some new ones.

"Are you paying me for this or are we doing it together?" Will had asked.

"What do you mean doing it together?"

"I mean are we partners, or what?"

"Why should we be partners?" Felipe asked him. "I got the job." He couldn't believe this jodido sometimes and felt his good mood slipping away. "I tell you what," he said, "I'll give you three hundred dollars when we're done, and that's it."

"So, this means if I get the next job, I can pay you what I think is right and keep the rest."

For a minute, Felipe just stared. Then he said, "What next one?"

That had happened thirty some years ago, and for all those years the two of them had worked one job after another. They built small houses in the mountains and additions in the village and garages and sheds and laid foundations and built decks and put on new roofs and plastered walls and set fence posts and built fireplaces and laid wood floors and messed with old sewer and plumbing lines. And through it all, although they complained about each other constantly, they somehow stuck together. It had been just four months ago that Felipe had told Will he was going to take some time off.

"I don't know how long," he said. He was staring off at a chained-up dog lying not far from the trailer they'd been working on. Patches of fur were missing on its belly and legs, one ear was gone, a trail of pus ran from its eyes, and it was staked where there was little shade. Felipe wondered why anyone would keep an animal like that.

"Maybe for a few months," he went on. "Maybe longer." He kicked a stone, and it flew off to where the dog was lying. "I guess I should tell you that if things go okay, I might be done for good."

He told Will that now that Elena had found a job in Las Sombras that paid pretty good, and that the loan to their house was finally paid off, he couldn't think of one good reason to keep on working like some kind of dumb animal that didn't know any better. Or, worse, like that Ramon Pacheco, an old man who the summer before had not only suffered a heart attack carrying a roll of roofing paper up a ladder, but had then fallen, tangled in the rungs of the ladder, into a bunch of hollyhocks swarming with bees.

"Besides," he went on, "I'm sick of doing the same thing every damn day. Even if it's different, it's still the same. This way I can finish working on my house and take my grandchildren fishing and work in my garden without running off to some jobsite. And maybe, since my back won't hurt from all the digging we do, me and Elena can have a good time together before we get too old." He took his hands out of his pockets and ran them up and down his arms, like he was cold. He looked over at Will. "It doesn't sound so bad, does it?" he said.

"No, it doesn't. Besides, you deserve it."

"I do, don't I?"

"Yes," Will said, thinking he should have seen this coming. There'd been a sour edge to Felipe ever since last winter, ever since Elena had begun working in Las Sombras. And although Will had noticed it, he hadn't taken it all that seriously. After all, the man always complained about everything, from the weather to his neighbors to the cost of lumber. But now that he thought about it, Will realized it was a little bit like the end of a marriage where, over time, one person makes things so bad that disappearing comes easy. Will wondered what it would be like to not have Felipe around. At least, he thought, it'll be quieter.

"You're sure about this?" Will asked.

"No," Felipe said. "Who can be sure about anything? But I'll try it and see what happens. Elena thinks it's a good idea."

"Well," Will said.

"Don't worry, hombre." Felipe said. "It's not like I'm dead. If you need some help, you know where I live. And if anybody calls, I'll pass your name on to them." He gave Will a push with the flat of his hand. "Venga," he said. "I brought some beer to celebrate."

They sat on the tailgate of Felipe's truck. It was a late afternoon in early May. The sun was still warm, the trees behind the trailer were leafed out. The wind, after blowing hard for the past two months, was still.

"I don't think I'm going to miss this too much," Felipe said, drinking from his beer and swinging his legs a little. "I always liked starting a job and finishing it up, but I never liked all that stuff in the middle." He looked over at Will. "We did a lot of jobs together," he said.

"We did," Will said, raising his beer. "It was a lot of years."

"You know which one was the best?"

"I know which one you liked the best," Will said. "The one where that woman was lying around naked."

"I was okay with that job," Felipe said, nodding. "How can you not like going to work when one minute you think it's just laying out a foundation, and the next someone's taking off all their clothes?"

"Yeah," Will said, smiling. He remembered Felipe carrying a bunch of 2x4s with one eye on where he was walking, and the other tracking the woman stretched out in the sun on a lawn chair. "That was a long time ago," he said.

"Seems like yesterday to me," Felipe said. "The worst job we ever did seems like yesterday to me, también. You remember that one?"

"Yes," Will said, "I remember that one, too."

Felipe snorted and finished off his beer. "You should know," he said. "It was all your fault we got stuck with it. I almost quit working with you after that, hombre. Everybody told me to just let you do it alone, let you freeze your ass off by yourself. I don't know how many times I told you not to take a job in December." He belched loudly, tossed the empty can back in the bed of the pickup, and popped open another one.

"But, no," he went on, "you don't listen to nothing."

"I listened," Will said. "I was just too broke to hear. It's not like I had a bunch of family around to feed me."

"Oh sí, blame it on me. Just because you've got no family means I get to be out in the cold all winter. You remember how the trees cracked?"

"Yes," Will said, "I remember." It had been so cold that winter that tree limbs had been frozen solid for weeks, and when they snapped it sounded like gunshots. It had been so cold that it had hurt to breathe the air, and no matter how many layers of clothes Will had worn, the cold still bit into his skin.

"That was one bad winter," Felipe said. "I'm glad I don't have that to worry about anymore. Now when it gets cold, I can think of you out there while I sit by the stove and drink some whiskey." He watched as the chained-up dog rose to its feet. It took a couple of steps and then, with a deep groan, sank back to the ground.

"That's the ugliest dog I've ever seen," Felipe said.

Will took a drink from his beer and looked over at the dog. Its water bowl was lying upside down in the dirt. "You think it got that way by itself?" he said.

"I don't know how it got that way," Felipe said. "All I know is it's one ugly dog."

Other than cows and sheep, no one in Guadalupe seemed to care much about animals. Dogs were kept chained or ran in packs, and if you were smart you kept clear of them. It wasn't all that much different from the farm country Will came from. Maybe dogs weren't chained there so much, but if they made one little mistake they were shot. He remembered a neighbor going outside one night in his underwear and shooting his dog for barking at nothing.

"We ought to give it some water," he said.

"Oh sí," Felipe said. "You give him some water. He's just waiting for someone to come close."

"Look at him," Will said. "He's probably dying of thirst."

"So?" Felipe said. "He's not my dog. He'd probably be happier being dead, anyway. What do you want to do, go water every dog in the village?"

Will shook his head. "All I'm saying," he began.

"Here," Felipe said. "Take a beer and forget about that dog." He leaned back a little, his hands behind him. "You know what I think?" he said. "I don't think I'll miss arguing with you. I think it'll be nice and peaceful to get up every morning and spend my day with people who agree with me and like to hear what I have to say."

"I bet," Will said, opening his beer and taking a drink. He thought that for a man he'd once seen arguing with a fence post for being in his way, he was setting his sights a little bit high. On top of that, while he didn't doubt that Felipe loved his wife and his grandchildren and his garden, he'd worked with him long enough to know that, other than his garden, he loved them a whole lot more when they weren't around. "I'll bet that'll be nice," he said again, and he took another long drink from his beer.

Will parked next to Felipe's truck, climbed out, and looked around. He hadn't been over here for a few months, and not much looked different. The portal Felipe was working on was still no more than a few standing posts with two by fours nailed up high to keep them from falling over. The outside plaster that Felipe had sworn he was going to color coat before winter was still gray and cracked. Even the junk pile of leftover lumber and rolls of wire and roofing paper and cinder blocks and spilled cardboard boxes of nails was the same. For a guy who'd said he'd have so much time to get things done, not much had happened. As he closed the door to his truck, he heard Felipe's voice.

"Hey, jodido, I'm over here."

Will found Felipe standing in the middle of his garden. He was wearing a frayed straw hat and irrigation boots, and since the ground was bone dry, Will had no idea why he had those on. A shovel was spaded in the dirt beside him, and in front of him was a small bucket half full of little potatoes.

"Hey," Will said.

"Hey yourself," Felipe said.

"What's with the boots?"

Felipe shrugged. "One of the kids was playing with my shoes, and who knows where they are now."

"Well," Will said, and smiled. "It's good to see you."

Felipe stared at him for a moment without speaking. That morning, all eight of his grandchildren had stormed the house at dawn for the pancakes that his wife made for them once a week before work. Not only had they come into his bedroom to see what he was doing, which was lying in bed staring up at the ceiling and wishing that everyone would just go away, but they had then proceeded to all talk at the same time about different things. When he complained to his wife about this, she gave him a look and said, "And just where do you think they get that?" After all of them had finally gone their separate ways, he'd washed the dishes, wiped the table and counters clean, and then gone outside to harvest his potatoes, which he discovered were not much bigger than marbles. And now, here was Will, who hadn't bothered to visit in months, popping up out of nowhere. Although, in truth, he was happy to see Will, he also thought it would have been nice to have a few moments of peace before two of his grandchildren reappeared at noon from that Headstart they went to.

"I'm in a bad mood," he said.

"I can see that," Will said and looked around at the garden. Even though it was late September, it wasn't hard to see that Felipe's crops hadn't done so well. The corn against the far fence was no higher than his waist, the squash were small and yellowed and burnt, and though the chilis had grown to a decent size it looked like they'd never flowered.

"My garden didn't do so good," Felipe said.

"No," Will said. "It doesn't look like it."

Felipe grunted. "We got that little rain in June and then nothing. On top of that, the ditch dried up in July. Everything baked in the sun all summer. Nothing can grow that way." He waved an arm at some shriveled plants threaded through string. "The peas were pretty good, but that was back in May. So long ago I barely remember."

The last five or six years had been dry. Sometimes just enough rain to give everybody a little hope, or just enough snow for people to think there might be a decent runoff. But for the most part, the whole area had slid into drought. It was only luck that there hadn't been a fire.

"Maybe next year," Will said.

Felipe spit out some air. "Oh sí," he said. "There's always next year." He pulled the shovel out of the ground and walked over to Will. "You want some coffee?" he offered.

"No," Will said, shaking his head. "I'm running way late. I came over to ask a favor. I want you to take a look at something."

"What kind of something?"

"Something I found. I don't want to tell you. I want you to see for yourself. It's over at Manuela García's place."

"Manuela García? How'd you end up with her? I've never known her to ask for help from anyone."

"I thought you might have told her to call me."

"No," Felipe said. "I never talked to her."

Will shrugged. "Well, she asked me," he said. "You got the time?"

"That's about all I've got," Felipe said. He could feel his bad mood lifting a little and thought that it wouldn't be so bad taking a ride with Will. "I have to be back by noon to watch the kids."

"No problem," Will said. "So let's go."

"So, how's your family?" Felipe asked. He was sitting on the passenger side of Will's truck, leaning back against the seat, one foot up on the edge of the dash. The window was open. His arm was hanging down the outside of the door, and every so often he'd lift his hand and let it play with the breeze. "I haven't seen Estrella for a long time," he said.

Just up ahead was Felix's Café. The Mexican, Ambrosio, was outside sweeping dirt into a thick cloud of dust, like he thought that if he got it into the air it might blow away. For all Felipe could tell, he was making one big mess of the outside of the cafe windows. He wondered if this was a trick Ambrosio had learned in Mexico or of it was something he'd picked up living in Guadalupe. He lived in a small trailer behind the cafe and sometimes helped Pepe cook in the kitchen. Every Saturday, late in the afternoon, Ambrosio would dress up in new blue jeans and a black button down shirt and pointed cowboy boots and walk to Tito's Bar and drink too much and sing sad songs. Felipe had been there a couple of times when Ambrosio had begun singing and he, along with everybody else, except Felix Sanchez, had left. None of them wanted to be around when the Mexican stopped his singing and began weeping about the family he'd left behind.

"Estrella's good," Will said, waving a hand at Ambrosio, who just stood there staring as they drove by. "The girls are getting bigger. School's started. Emilia's a pain in the ass. But what else is new." He glanced over at Felipe, who was staring straight ahead out the windshield. "Let me ask you something," he said. "Did you ever hear anything about all the Raels being Jews?"

Felipe wondered how one minute everything seemed normal and the next Will was asking about some girl found hanging from a bridge or who was the black man who had lived here that no one remembered or, like now, whether all the Raels were Jews. He looked over at Will.

"Where'd you hear that?" he said.

"Estrella told me. Her grandmother told her all the Raels are Jews and have kept it secret."

Felipe knew Carmela Rael. She was sort of old even when he was a boy. Every autumn, he and his friends would cut through her property to hunt rabbits in the foothills, and when she would see them, she would yell and throw rocks at them. And she didn't throw like a girl, either. He remembered Rudy once getting hit so hard in the head that he fell face first in the dirt and laid there without moving. He remembered standing beside him not knowing what to do, and then remembered Carmela Rael walking quickly toward them, shaking her head and talking to herself. But he couldn't remember what had happened after that. Did the old woman throw rocks at him or did he run away? And just what had happened to Rudy?

Whatever happened, he thought, must have been so bad that I have a blank spot. I'll have to ask Rudy about this when I see him.

"So," Will said. "What do you think?"

"About what?"

Will shook his head."About the Raels being Jewish."

"How should I know," Felipe said. "But what is she, a hundred years old? And you're going to believe what she says? A hundred years ago all they had was donkeys. They didn't even know what a car was. And now she thinks all the Raels are Jews?"

"Yeah," Will said, wondering why he ever asked Felipe anything. "I'll tell Estrella that. That'll make her feel better."

They drove by Tito's Bar. Just past that, Will could see Joe Vigil outside the lumberyard talking to Lloyd Romero. As they drove by, Lloyd grinned and threw both arms up in the air.

"Fucking Lloyd," Felipe said. "Standing around waiting for something to happen so he can tell everyone." He dropped his foot and pushed up straight on the seat. He could feel his bad mood coming back.

"You know what I don't know?" he said. "I don't know why people have so many kids. When they're little all they do is want things, and you have to do everything for them. You've got to feed them and wipe their butts and get up in the middle of the night and sit there and pat their backs. I don't get it. All they are is work. Then, when they get bigger, they think they know everything, and the next thing you know they're dumping their own kids on you. It's one big waste of time."

Will slowed down for a couple of dogs crossing the highway, and then turned off onto a dirt road. "I think the idea," he said, "is that when you get old, it's their turn to take care of you."

Felipe grunted. He raised his arm and smacked the outside of the truck door. "So, you think there's a plan?" he said. "Maybe with girls there is. Girls always have a plan, even if it's bad. But I bet you when I get old, my boys will stick me under a tree and feed me leftovers."

Will looked over at him. "I can tell you're having a good time not working."

Felipe shrugged and waved a hand. "It's not so bad," he said, "when no one's around."

Manuela García was outside her house when they drove up. She was standing in the shade beneath a cottonwood tree by the ditch, and wearing the same black dress she'd worn when Will had first met her. Her hair was tied back, and the sight of her made him think of old photographs he'd come across. Those photographs of women standing on dusty roads, or before an empty church, or a glimpse of them through an open doorway. In every one there had been that same hard, rigid look that he now saw on Manuela García's face.

"Manuela García," Felipe said, leaning forward in the cab. "I haven't seen her for a long time. She got old."

Will pulled to a stop and shut off the engine. "Do you know her?" he asked.

"No," Felipe said. "Not really. In this village there's family and friends, and then those others that you see sometimes. You think you know them just because they're here, but you don't. She's one of those." He wiped the inside of the windshield and leaned close to it. "Her house doesn't look so bad. What are you doing in there?"

"It's not that house," Will said. He was beginning to feel uncomfortable sitting in the truck with Felipe while the old woman stood there staring. He pointed out the side window. "It's that old place up the hill," he said.

Felipe turned his head and looked out the open window.

"You're working on that?" he said. The place looked like it had been abandoned for decades. The door hung open, the roof sagged, and the north wall bulged out like it was on the verge of collapse. There was an empty, hollow feel to it that Felipe felt would never be gone, no matter how much work Will put into it.

"Why don't you just take it down?" Felipe said. Or better yet, he thought, let it fall over and forget all about it.

"Don't even start," Will said, and he pushed open the truck door.

Felipe got out of the pickup and walked over to Manuela García. "Cómo está, Mrs. García?" he said. "I haven't seen you for a long time."

The old woman looked smaller to Will than she had before and a little out of place, like there wasn't much of her inside the dress she was wearing, and as if it had been a long time since she'd stepped out of her house. She moved her eyes to Will.

"I was waiting for you," she said. "You're late, and it's only the second day."

"I know," Will said. "I'm sorry. I got hung up with my kids."

"Why is he here?" she asked, without even a glance at Felipe.

"I asked him to help me move that old cookstove. It's too heavy to move alone."

Manuela wrapped her arms across her chest, as if a chill had run through her. "You could leave it where it is."

"I could," Will said. "But I thought we agreed to empty the place out."

For a moment, no one spoke. And then Manuela García finally looked at Felipe. "You're that Griego boy, aren't you?" she said.

"Yes," Felipe said. "My father was Octaviano Griego. My mother is..."

"I know who your mother is," Manuela said. "I remember stories about her."

Felipe pulled his head back slightly. He asked, "What kind of stories?"

"The kind I'm sure were not true," Manuela said, and smiled. "You used to work with mi hijo, didn't you?"

For a second, Felipe wasn't sure who she was talking about, and then realized she meant Will. "Yes," he said. "Will and I worked together for a long time."

"Do you think I made a mistake to hire him?"

"No," Felipe said. "He knows what he's doing, and he's honest."

"Do you think he'll need your help after this?"

Felipe glanced up the hill at the old house, and then looked back at Manuela. He knew this old woman wasn't asking a question. "No," he said. "I don't think so."

"Bueno," she said. "I'm glad to hear that. You tell your mother I said hello." And then she turned and walked slowly away.

Will watched her for a bit, wondering at what had happened. Then he looked over at Felipe who was staring back at him and smiling a little.

"Good luck with her, jodido," he said. "I think you're going to need it." Then he shook his head. "I'm just glad I don't work with you anymore."

"I don't know if you caught that, Will," Felipe said, "but it's one thing to say, 'how are you, hijo', and it's another to call someone their hijo to someone else. How long have you been hanging out with this woman?"

"Not long enough to be part of her family," Will said.

"Well, you better make sure she knows that or you'll end up moving in with her." They were making their way up the slope through the sagebrush. The old house was about fifty yards away. There was a narrow trail leading up the hill, but Felipe could tell that other than Will and maybe skunks no one had walked it for a long, long time.

"Who built this place, anyway?" he asked.

"I don't know," Will said, pushing aside branches and then holding on to them so they didn't snap back at Felipe. "Manuela told me it was her grandfather's house, but she said it might have been here even before then. You've never been here before?"

"No," Felipe said, and then thought there was even something weird about that. As a kid, he'd run all over the village, along the creeks and ditches, and up and down the foothills, but he couldn't remember ever stumbling across this old house. In fact, it didn't even make sense for it to be here. Most of the old houses in Guadalupe were crowded around the church or in the valley not far from it. He couldn't think of one good reason why someone would have built a house so long ago up on a slope where there was no pasture and no water and no people.

"So what are you supposed to do with it?" he asked.

"She wants it to look the way it did when she was a young girl, and she wants it done before she dies. But I'm figuring on a new roof, get rid of the rotten wood, and plaster it. I'm not sure what she wants done on the inside."

"And she's going to pay you for this?"

"I told her it was a waste of time and money, but you see how she is."

Felipe stepped over a mound of dirt swarming with red ants. "I saw, all right," he said.

When they got to the old house, the sun was high and hot, the air a little hazed. Felipe went over to the trash Will had piled up. "There was a bed in there?" he said.

"Just the frame and the springs," Will said. "No mattress."

Felipe bent over and moved a broken chair out of the way. He picked up a piece of clothing, holding it away from him with two fingers. It was a man's coat. It smelled of rot and piss and filth. He shook it a little, enough that he could see it would have fit a man, maybe not taller than him and Will, but one thicker. He looked at Will. "Her grandfather?"

Will shrugged. "Your guess is as good as mine," he said. Felipe tossed it back on the pile. "Not much worth anything, is there?" he said.

"No," Will said. "Some old shelving, the bed, an old stove, some trash, and that table. Most of it was broken like someone had trashed the place. Manuela thought people may have taken things, but I don't think there ever was much of anything in there."

Felipe walked over to the west side of the house. The sage wasn't so tall there, and he could see that the ground was sunk in a little, the stub ends of old posts and a rusted piece of metal sticking out of the dirt. "This is where the house came from," he said. "They dug up the dirt, made adobe bricks out of it, and then filled the hole back in with garbage and whatever else they didn't need. Who knows what's under there."

"Like an old Indian burial ground," Will said.

"But I bet there's no pot shards in there." Felipe looked up the hill at the piñon, at the two ropes dangling from an upper limb, and hissed out some air. "That's an old swing up there," he said.

"I know. I saw it yesterday."

"So there were kids up here."

"You know what?" Will said. "I just work here, and this is my second day. I have no idea what was up here."

Beyond the piñon, a stretch of sage led up to a line of trees. Past that were the foothills, the slopes loose rock and scattered piñon and juniper trees. "Maybe this was a pasture once," he said. "And when everybody left, the sage took over."

"There's still no water."

Felipe shook his head. "That's right," he said. "There's still no water." He looked over at Will. "So, what do you want me to look at?"

Even with all the doors and windows left open all night, the inside of the house still smelled bad. Felipe knew that no matter how long the place was aired out, the stench of mold and damp that had sunk into the walls would never be completely gone. The dirt floor was rough and uneven, and light filtered through spaces between the wood of the roof.

"It's in here," Will said, and he led Felipe into the middle room. It took a few seconds for his eyes to adjust before he could make out what he'd found the day before.

"There," he said, pointing. "Down low. Tell me what you think they are."

Felipe wasn't listening. He was standing in the entrance to the last room. The east door and the window across from it were open, and sun was spilling in. A rusted cookstove sat in far corner. The room had been swept, and hanging on all four walls were hundreds of crosses. They made the room look smaller than it was, as if the walls were crowding in. A wave of vertigo swept over Felipe and then was gone. He shook his head and took a step back.

"What is this?" he asked.

Will had been so preoccupied with what was in the wall that he'd forgotten about the crosses. He took a step over to Felipe and looked into the room. It was flooded with light, much more than the day before, and he could see cobwebs woven in the crosses, and the dust that lay on them.

"They're crosses," Will said.

"I know they're crosses," Felipe said. "What are they doing here?" It reminded him of some of the homes in Guadalupe that were covered with pictures of Jesus and saints printed on flat pieces of tin and carved santos and candles and plastic flowers and crucifixes, but that was something else. He'd never seen anything quite like this. On the wall across from him, he could see that one was made of the skinned limbs from a juniper tree. The branches had been carved and were twisted together, as if whoever had made it had forced things into a place they didn't want to go.

"What are they doing here?" he asked.

"I don't know what they're doing here," Will said.

"Did you tell Manuela about this?"

"Yes. She told me to get rid of all of them."

Felipe looked over at Will. "She knew they were here?"

"No," Will said. "She told me she didn't know about them. She told me she had no idea what was in this house."

Felipe shook his head. "Well," he said. "I can see why you wanted to show me this. But I don't know what to tell you." He thought that there wasn't one thing religious about any of them, and that someone not in their right mind had made them. Manuela was right. They should be hauled out and burned.

Will grunted and smiled a little. "I hate to tell you this," he said, "but that's not why I brought you up here." He took Felipe's arm and half turned him. "Down there," he said. "Take a look down there."

"Down where?" Felipe asked. "All I see is a wall." After looking into the sun in the other room, he was having trouble seeing anything. He blinked his eyes and narrowed them.

"You need to get closer," Will said. He stepped forward and squatted down. "It's right here."

Felipe stooped down beside Will, where he could just make out a series of narrow ridges protruding from the wall. He ran the flat of his hand over them and then, grunting, got down on his hands and knees and brought his face closer.

"Somebody stuck some sticks in the adobe," he said, more to himself than to Will. "Maybe to bless the house or for good luck or something."

"That's what I thought, too," Will said. "Look closer."

There were four of them, spaced evenly apart, a slight gap between them. "What else can they be?" Felipe muttered.

"You're supposed to tell me," Will said. "That's why you're here."

Once more, Felipe ran a hand over them. Then, with a fingernail, he scraped at one. He scraped until he could feel how hard it was, and until he could see the dull, white color of bone. And then he wiped his hand hard on his pants and sat back.

"Jesus Christ," he said. And he didn't want to be in this house any longer.

"There's someone buried in your wall," Felipe said, the palm of his hand still moving up and down his pants leg.

They were standing in the sun just past the trash pile, far enough away that Felipe could catch the scent of sage instead of the damp odor seeping out of the house. There was nothing moving down the hill, and Will could see that the curtains in Manuela's house were all drawn.

"It's not my wall," he said.

"Well then in Manuela García's wall. I don't care whose wall it is. There's somebody in it." He looked at his hand, and then again rubbed the palm of it hard down his leg. "I can't believe I was just messing with somebody's bones."

"You don't think it's something else?"

Felipe considered not even answering Will's stupid question, but then it occurred to him that soon he'd be going home, leaving Will to deal with all this. "No," he said. "Do you?"

Will shook his head. "No," he said. "I guess not. I was just hoping."

"Hoping for what? You knew what it was. You just wanted some company."

Will smiled a little. "Maybe you're right," he said. "Maybe I was getting a little lonely up here. But after all these years, you probably owe me one."

"I owe you one? You never were too good at counting, were you, Will?" He watched as Will pulled back slightly, and then, as if things weren't bad enough, he felt worse for making Will feel bad. He looked down at the ground and moved some dirt with the side of his boot. When he looked up, he said, "I think it's like this," and he cupped his right hand slightly and held it out. "What you found is the outside of someone's fingers. The thumb is probably tucked into his palm and the arm is further back in the wall."

"What if there isn't any more?"

Felipe stared at him. He had the sudden feeling that he'd been mistaken, that Will was too stupid to feel bad and had just been biding his time to ask yet another dumb question. "You mean somebody just stuck a hand in the wall? Why would somebody do that?"

"How should I know?" Will asked. "Why would someone put a body in their wall?"

Felipe shrugged his shoulders. "Maybe it was a bad winter and the ground was too hard to dig. Or maybe they cared about him too much and didn't want him too far away."

Will spit out a breath. "That's the only idea you can come up with?" he asked. "That they buried him in the bedroom so he'd be close? And why do you keep saying him? Maybe it's a woman."

For a few seconds, Felipe didn't say anything. He knew but didn't want to say that whoever was in the wall was someone small, like a child. And for some reason, the thought of it being a young girl felt worse to him. He shook his head.

"I don't know," he said. "It's just a way to talk. I don't know who's in there."

"Have you ever run into something like this?"

As a young boy, Felipe was always a little afraid of his grandmother on his father's side. While she fed him cookies and warm milk and made him shriveled up apple dolls like she thought he was a girl, she would also frighten him with stories of the village. She'd sit down at the kitchen table and tell him that when she was little the winters were so long and so cold and the ground so frozen that the dead were kept wrapped in blankets in Patricio Martinez's chicken coop and weren't buried until the earth thawed in the spring.

"And sometimes not even then, hijo," she'd tell him in a whisper. "Sometimes one or two of the dead would be missing, usually it was one of those Garcías, but still. It was as if they had gotten up and walked away, like they didn't like being dead or were tired of waiting. And who knows where they went wrapped in their rags."

She told him that priests were buried in the floor of the church, even the bad ones, like that Father Donaldo, who used to beat his donkey with a stick until it bawled like a baby, and that many of the old houses had their own graveyards where infants and old people were buried.

"Many of the markers are gone now," she told him, "so it's hard to know where they are. But you must always be careful where you walk. And remember, hijo, just because they're dead doesn't mean there isn't a little bit of them left behind." After her stories, she would take the plates to the sink and wipe the table of crumbs while Felipe sat there quietly staring straight ahead. Then she would put an arm around her grandson's shoulders and lean close to the side of his face.

"And remember, mi hijo, never ever go near Patricio Martinez's chicken coop."

But, Felipe now thought, for all her stories, not once had she ever mentioned anyone being buried in the wall of their house.

"No," he said to Will. "I've never heard of this one before."

"So, what do you think we should do?"

Felipe snorted and jerked back his head. "What do you mean we, jodido. I just came because you wanted to show me. This is your job, not mine."

"All right, all right. So what should I do?"

"I don't know," Felipe said, slowly. "I guess you could dig out whoever it is and bury him somewhere. Or maybe just plaster over him and forget all about it." He bent over and picked up a stone and tossed it down the hill. He watched as it struck a branch of sage and kicked up a little puff of dust.

"Or maybe," he said, "you could just go home and never come back." Then, after a long pause, he shook his head. "I don't know what you should do."

They didn't talk much on the ride back to Felipe's. Manuela's house was quiet when they left, the curtains still drawn. They drove by Bernabe Medina's place. The old man was outside, and this time he lifted a hand as they went by. When Will asked what he was going to do with the rest of his day, Felipe shrugged and said he'd promised to take all eight of his grandchildren fishing at the river after school. And that he must not have been thinking when he made that promise. The last time he'd taken them, the half that wanted to fish kept getting their lines tangled, and the ones that didn't either threw rocks in the river where their cousins were fishing, or fell in. And after about an hour of that, they'd all left in bad moods.

"What I really want to do," he said, "is go take a nap. And maybe then I can forget I ever took this ride with you."

When they pulled into Felipe's drive and stopped, Felipe looked over at Will. "Pues," he said. "I never thought I'd have this kind of a morning." Then he grunted softly and got out of the pickup. He closed the truck door and leaned over, looking in the open window.

"You want to come in for a beer?" he asked.

"I better not," Will said, shaking his head. "It's a little too early for that."

"So, what are you going to do?"

"Hell if I know," he said. He already felt as though the day was lost. The thought of walking back up to the old García house without any idea of just what to do was exhausting.

"You could tell Manuela about this," Felipe said. "Let her figure it out. It's her house. It's probably her relative in there. Who else could it be?" He straightened up. "And get rid of those crosses," he said. "I don't even like thinking of them."

"Yeah," Will said. "I will." He slapped the steering wheel and put the truck into gear. "I'll see you later," he said, and eased his foot off the clutch.

## SIX

⚹ THROUGH A SMALL CRACK in the kitchen curtains, Manuela García watched Will and Felipe walk down the hill from her grandfather's house. She had stood there all morning, the muscles in her legs straining, her arms crossed tight across her chest, watching. She'd seen Felipe push at the bedframe with his foot and then wander over to the old pit in front of the house, and she knew he knew that the walls of her grandfather's house had come from there.

She waited while they were inside the house and then watched them come out of the house and move away from it and talk. Just a little ways beyond them, one of the ropes hanging from the piñon tree began to sway gently. Her breath caught in her chest, and she felt her heart begin to beat a little faster.

Look behind you, hijo, she thought, her head trembling a little, her fingers digging into her arms. She didn't care about the other one, that Griego boy. She didn't care what he saw.

Look behind you. There's not a breath of wind, yet the rope is moving. If you turned and saw it, you would begin to wonder. But a part of her knew he would never see it. If he did, he would think it was a breeze he hadn't noticed, or that an

87

animal had brushed against it, or that it was nothing at all. He had just begun work in that house. It was still too soon for him to know anything.

They finished their talk and began to walk down the hill, Will coming first and the other one following behind. When they passed out of sight, she left the kitchen and hurried to the front door, which she had left open. She stood just inside the doorway and watched the two men climb into the truck and start the engine. She stood there as it turned onto the dirt road and a few seconds later disappeared among the trees. Then all that was left of them was a soft haze of dust that the tires had kicked up, hanging in the air.

He won't be back, she thought. He may think he will, but he won't. He'll take that Griego man home to wherever he lives and then the two of them will drink their beer and their whiskey like every other man in this village.

A sudden fatigue shot through her. She reached out for the doorframe to steady herself and lowered her head. Below the hem of her dress, she could see the pale white color of her legs and the veins running dark beneath the skin. Her feet were bare and seemed to be all bone, the skin cracked and flaking, her toes twisted and misshapen. I've grown old, she thought. So old all I have left is a man who will never come back to me.

When she raised her eyes, other than the dust having settled, not one thing had changed outside. The sun still shone hot and the leaves on the cottonwood trees were as dull and listless and still as before. She pushed off the frame and stood up straight. And then she turned, opened the door closest to her, and stepped into her bedroom.

Across from the bed, one window looked out on the trees that ran along the ditch. Beside the bed was a tall bureau where she kept her clothes and in one drawer some of the things her grandfather had given her when she was little. The floor was hardwood planks covered here and there with small rugs. The ceiling was hand-hewn beams covered with boards. Sometimes when the wind blew or the ants were moving about, the dirt above them would sift through the cracks and fall onto her bed, onto the floor, onto the clothes she left lying about.

Like the other rooms in the house, there was nothing hanging on the walls. But standing on the bureau was a santo that stood only eight inches high, carved out of cottonwood in the image of a young boy. He stood with his arms at his sides, his head bowed slightly. His eyes were open and looking down. His chest was thin and hollowed out and bare. His hair and his hand and his feet had once been painted black, but the color had long ago cracked and faded. As a child, Manuela had often slept with him, and there were places on his body and face that had been rubbed smooth by her fingers. It was her grandfather who had given him to her.

"I have brought you something, hija," he had said, walking into her bedroom. Even though it was summer, he wore a heavy coat and boots. He was unshaven, his hair disheveled, his eyes bloodshot and streaked with yellow. There was the smell of woodsmoke on him and something rancid, like lard gone bad.

"Where's my father?" the girl had asked.

"He's gone, Manuela," the old man said. "I've sent him away." He went to the bed and sat down, his weight so heavy she could hear the coiled springs give. He unbuttoned his coat and threw it off.

"Come sit by me," he said. And when she did, he placed the santo in her lap and pulled her closer. "It's for you, mi hija, so you always remember." His hand had gone to the ribbon in her hair, and he untied it slowly.

Now, Manuela walked to her bed and unfastened the buttons to her dress. She let it slide off her shoulders and fall to the floor, and then, carefully, she stepped over it. She undid her hair, letting it fall loose down her back. Then she pulled back the quilt, lay down and covered herself. She folded her hands together on her belly and closed her eyes. She let her thoughts drift from one thing to another, and when the old house up the hill pushed itself into her mind, she looked for something, anything, to take her somewhere else. And this time, this late morning, it was Rosalie.

At first, all Manuela saw was Rosalie's face, or what she thought was her sister's face. After all, what she remembered had been eighty years before when Manuela was five years old and Rosalie not yet two. Manuela remembered the sound of the wind and the cold that blew through the cracks around the windows and doors. She remembered the feel of her sister's body lying small and hot against hers and the sight of her mother's hands reaching down. And later, she remembered waking alone in the house her mother and sister had left.

"Come, Rosalie," Josefina had said. She spoke softly so as not to wake Manuela. The light in the room came from a smoke-stained lantern on top of a chest filled with old quilts. Josefina's daughters were sleeping in the same bed. Manuela was on her back, her head turned slightly, her lips parted. Rosalie lay close against her, her face against her sister's shoulders, both arms tucked beneath her. Her skin was flushed and her breath came so quickly that Josefina could see the rapid rise and fall of the blankets.

Her daughters had been sick for days with fever and a deep, harsh cough. While Manuela's illness had lessened, Rosalie's had only grown worse. No matter what Josefina had done, Rosalie's cough had remained dry and tight, her fever so high that her eyelids and lips had blistered. But what frightened Josefina even more was that earlier that day she had glimpsed a dullness in her daughter's eyes that she had not noticed before.

"Rosalie is not getting better," she had told her husband, and as soon as the words came from her mouth, she knew she was afraid.

"She will be fine," her husband told her, his voice slurred, his gaze somewhere else, somewhere distant. His eyes were bloodshot and glazed, and were that way even when he did not drink. Josefina often thought something that had once been inside of him had been taken away and what was left was dull and slow-witted, like some animal that had been beaten or left alone for too long.

He had been drinking since mid-day and now sat slumped at the kitchen table watching the snow fall outside the window. Every so often, a gust of wind would strike the house, shaking the panes of glass and sending up little puffs of smoke from the woodstove.

"Tomorrow," he said, nodding his head, and without looking at his wife. "She will be better tomorrow. You'll see."

"No," Josefina said. "That is what you said yesterday and the day before. Tomorrow she will be worse."

He raised a hand as if to slap the top of the table, and then he let it fall almost gently. "I will talk to my father," he said. "Is that what you want?"

For a moment, Josefina did not answer. It was getting dark now, and every so often, through the snow, she caught a glimpse of light coming from the house up on the slope. It seemed to move from one room to another, as if her father-in-law was pacing back and forth through the three rooms.

For the most part, her husband's father kept to himself, but there were times when he came down the hill to bring them meat, a deer he had shot or a calf he had stolen from the village. Sometimes he came with a burlap bag stuffed with clothes or a small wooden box full of odd stones and marbles and coins rubbed smooth. And those times, he would stare outright at

Josefina and, later, at her two daughters. And then he would look over at his son.

"Go into the woods," he would tell him. "Go into the woods and don't come back here until I leave." And then, after his son had left, he would look at Josefina again, and in a harsh voice he would say, "Put the girls in their room."

And after Josefina's husband had disappeared into the woods and the girls were in their room, he would take Josefina roughly by the arm and lead her to the bed where she slept with his son. The first time this happened, she had been fifteen years old. She had been married less than a month and was so startled and frightened by what was happening that she had done little more than whimper when her husband's father raised her dress and pushed her to the bed and, with the flat of his hands, spread her legs. After that, she fought him soundlessly until he raised his hand, and then, as if she had become him, she would raise her own dress and lie down on the bed. And later, after the birth of her daughters and especially when she would hear Manuela calling for her or Rosalie crying, she would close her eyes and say softly, "I'm here, mi hijas," and then almost in a frenzy, she would grab the old man by the hips and pull him deeper inside her. "Hurry," she would whisper harshly.

Now, she stared across the room at her husband and said, "No, that's not what I want." It was almost dark outside, and Josefina could hear the wind growing stronger, blowing so hard that nothing could be seen of the house up on the hill. The wood in the stove had burned low, and a chill was filling the room.

"I want you to go to the village and find the midwife," she said. "I want you to tell her how sick our daughter is and beg her to come here."

"It's snowing, Josefina," her husband said. "And it has been for days. The path to the village is gone and, besides, no one would come here on a night like this." And then he pushed back his chair and stood up slowly.

He is like an old man, Josefina thought. An old man of no use to anyone. She watched as he raised his eyes and looked at her.

"She will be better in the morning," he said. Then he walked by her, brushing against her shoulder, and went into the bedroom. And within minutes, Josefina heard the sounds of his uneasy sleep.

She left the kitchen and hurried to her daughter's room, to the side of the bed where they slept. "Come, Rosalie," she whispered, reaching down. Manuela stirred, and then, as Josefina lifted Rosalie from the bed, she moaned and stretched out a hand for her sister. "Hush, Manuela," her mother told her. "Go to sleep." She pulled the blanket up to Manuela's chin and soothed her until her breathing eased.

As quietly as possible, Josephina moved the lantern from the chest and took out a heavy quilt which she threw around her shoulders. She took out another, smaller one and covered Rosalie until only her face could be seen. Then, for a moment, Josefina just stood there quietly. She could feel the heat from Rosalie's body burning beneath the quilt. She could hear the wind and the vigas overhead settling from the weight of the snow. And beneath all that, she could hear Manuela's soft breath.

"Sleep, mi hija," she said, her voice little more than air, "and before you know it your sister and I will be back." Then, wrapping the quilt tightly around herself and Rosalie, she left the room and went to the door that led outside. The moment she opened it, a wave of snow and wind and cold swept over her and Rosalie began to cry.

At that time, the priest in the village of Guadalupe was Father Joseph. He had been priest there for so long that he'd come to forget there had ever been a life before this one.

Vaguely, he remembered a place of bright sun and endless water and white, winding roads. He remembered nuns shrouded in black and bent from age who spoke in a language he had now forgotten. But the memory of it all was so distant that he was often confused as to whether it came from his own life or from some book of pictures he may have seen as a child.

In the years he had been priest in Guadalupe, he had married and baptized and buried so many that he had come to feel as if time had swept everyone from one place to another and left him standing alone, as if he were a stone stuck in a fast current. That all he had to show for his life was old age and illness and a growing sense of sadness that seemed to come from everywhere, from the sight of the bowed heads when he spoke Mass, from the stillness of the mountains at dawn, from knowing that he understood so little as his life was nearing an end, from the sight of the heavy snow falling outside the church window.

The priest was standing before one of the long, narrow windows set in the thick wall of the church. He was dressed in a coat buttoned tight at the neck and a hat that covered his ears and in rubber boots that came almost to his knees. On his hands were wool mittens that smelled faintly of lanolin. The old woman who cleaned the church had been ill for days, and Father Joseph had taken it upon himself to wipe the dust from each station of the cross and brush away the dirt and bits of straw that had fallen from the high ceiling overhead onto the surface of the altar. It had taken him all afternoon and into the evening to do these few chores, and now it had been dark outside for hours.

He was not looking forward to the walk home. Although it was cold inside the church, he knew how bitter it would be outside. Through the fog his breath made on the glass, he could see that the snow had drifted high against the wall of the church and that the path to his small house was gone.

He shook his head and felt a sharp pain bite deep into his stomach. He grunted and moved a hand beneath his coat and pushed at it until, finally, it eased. It wasn't the first time he had felt this. It had begun the previous fall and was now so constant that the priest knew it would only get worse. He had grown thin over the past few months and what appetite he'd had was gone.

He let out a long, ragged breath and moved slowly away from the window. He went to the door, and with what seemed to be all his strength, pulled it open. He lowered his head as the wind and snow bit into his face.

The snow was high above the priest's knees, and after only thirty yards he was out of breath and had fallen twice and, worse, the ache in his belly had started up again. Although his house was not far away, he was beginning to think that he had been foolish to go out in such weather, that he should have stayed in the church and spent the night there. He glanced over his shoulder. The snow was falling so hard now that he could no longer see where he had come from. All he could make out about him was the dim shadow of the few houses and the branches of the cottonwood tree that stood not far away swaying in the wind. He took a few more steps forward, and that was when he caught sight of someone on the road walking toward him.

At first, he thought he must be mistaken, that no one would be out on a night like this. He thought that his eyes must be playing tricks on him, or that possibly some animal had jumped a fence or pushed through a gate and was now, like himself, wandering lost. His hands and feet were cold and wet from falling, and a sudden chill went through him, like the onset of a fever. The wind was growing stronger, and through the blowing snow, the priest could see that the figure moving toward him was closer, and he thought that by its size and by the way it moved, it must be a woman.

"What could be so important that someone would face this storm?" he wondered. And then he stumbled forward until the two of them were a few paces apart.

A snow-encrusted blanket was wrapped around the woman so that only her face was visible. One side of her face was swollen and bruised, as if someone had struck her or as if she had fallen against a tree or a rock. Her skin was burnt from the wind and spotted white in places from frost. Her eyebrows were iced, as was the hair that was exposed along each side of her face. Her belly swelled as if she was carrying something beneath the blanket, or as if, the priest thought, she might be full with child. Even in such a state, Father Joseph could see how young she was. He could also see that he had never seen her before in his life, and he had no idea how that could be.

"Who are you?" he asked, as if it mattered who she was or where she had come from. All that mattered was for the two of them to get to a sheltered place as soon as possible.

"Come, hija," he said, reaching out. "My house is not so far," and when he touched her arm, she moved her eyes toward him. They were bloodshot and streaked at the corners with ice.

"Who are you?" she said, her lips barely moving, as if it hurt her to speak, her voice so low that the priest could barely hear what she said. He moved yet a step closer.

"Mi hija," he said, again. "Come with me. There's nothing to fear. I am the priest of this village." He thought that if they did not get inside soon, they would freeze to death in this storm.

"I'm looking for something," the woman said, slowly, and now the priest could hear her words clearly. "But I've forgotten what it is."

"It's of no matter," he said. "What matters is that we get out of this weather. Come, my house is just a short distance from here." And as he took her arm a gust of wind blew so hard that he stumbled even closer to her, so close that he could see the frozen water beneath her eyes and the cracks in her lips filled with blood.

"No," she said, her voice suddenly sharp and bitter. "No! How many times do you think I can be with you, old man?" Her eyes were wide open, and she looked at him in such a way that he thought she must know him, that they must have met before. But where it could have been he didn't know. She pulled free of his hand and shook her head so hard that the quilt slid from her shoulders to the snow. Then, with one hand, she tore at the top of her shirt until the buttons ripped off, exposing the skin from her neck to just below her breasts.

"Get this from me," she said. "I am burning."

The shirt she was wearing was soaked through, and her dress clung cold and wet to her legs. The priest could see that she held an infant that was partly covered by a small blanket. The child's face was turned toward him.

My God, he thought. And then he saw that the child's face was the color of marble and that its eyes and mouth were still and half open. One arm had fallen free from the blanket, and when Father Joseph pulled off one of his mittens and touched it, the arm was as cold as ice.

"Hija," the priest said, and suddenly he wasn't sure who he was speaking to, this young woman who had appeared out of nowhere or the dead infant she held. He raised his eyes and looked at the woman's naked breasts, at how she still pulled at her shirt and thought that he should cover her, cover them both in case someone was to see. And if they did, what would they think? But instead, he felt a great weariness fall over him and he turned his head slowly and gazed past the two of them at the snow snaking across what was once a road, what was once a village. And when she said, "I have two daughters, and neither are yours," it came to him that the snow could have been sand that was blowing, fine, white sand thrown by the wind. And beyond all of it would be a sea of dark water that stretched forever.

He barely noticed as the woman stopped struggling and lifted her child and held her close. He barely heard her say, "Come, my sweet Rosalie. There is no help here. Your sister is waiting for us." And he was barely aware of her as she turned and walked away. The priest just stood where he was as she moved farther and farther away, the wind snatching at her dress, at her hair. And finally, she had gone so far that, if he had been watching, he would not have been able to see even a shadow of her. His belly was aching and, absently, he moved his bare hand beneath his coat. He wondered suddenly how long he had been standing in this storm. He wondered how long he had been in this village, and when it was that he had first come here. Off to the side, the wind whipped the branches of the cottonwood tree beside the church. And he felt as though he had been standing alone in the snow forever in a place he no longer recognized.

Manuela woke from her rest slowly, so slowly that at first she wasn't quite sure if she'd slept or if she had been lying in a state somewhere between wakefulness and sleep. If she had dreamed dreams, she had no memory of what they were.

The light in the room had shifted. Shadows were lying along the floor, and Manuela knew that it was late afternoon, that in not so long it would be dark. She sat up, swung her legs around and stood naked, keeping a hand on the bed for balance. Then she stepped into her dress and carefully worked it up her body. She straightened the quilt on the bed and smoothed the pillow, and then she looked at the small santo standing by itself on top of the dresser.

The boy had stood there nearly all her life, in this room, on her dresser. As a girl, she had carried him about with her.

He had sat with her while she ate meals with her father, and he had slept with her, and he had been with her when she went outside and played. Sometimes, she had dressed him in pieces of cloth and ribboned his head, and then she had talked to him as if he were a girl. Once, she had dug a shallow hole and buried him and left him there overnight. And that night, she'd lain awake thinking that he was outside all alone beneath the ground and that when she looked for him in the morning he might not be there or worms might have eaten into him or his eyes, instead of gazing down, would be staring at her, wondering why she had done such a thing to him.

But she hadn't so much as touched him for so long that, now, there was a thin layer of dust on his body and the wood just beneath still held a veneer of flaked varnish. Manuela walked around the bed, picked him up, and the two of them left the room.

The front door to the house was still open, and outside she could see that, even with no wind, the leaves on the cottonwood were beginning to fall. Soon, she thought, the limbs would be bare and the ground would freeze and there would be snow. And then there would be so many reasons for Will Sawyer not to come back. She closed her eyes, pressed the boy close to her chest, and shook her head.

"It's too soon for me to think that," she said, not bothering even to wonder if she was speaking to herself or to the boy. "Maybe later, but not now. Tomorrow. You'll see, he'll be back tomorrow."

She turned from the door, and made her way slowly through the house to the kitchen. Even though the room was growing dark there was still enough daylight seeping in around the curtains above the sink for her to see. She looked at the few pots hanging from hooks, at the towel hung neatly from the stove, at the one cup on the kitchen table. Then she stepped inside the room. She brought the cup to the sink, placed the boy on the windowsill, and, leaning forward on her toes, drew the curtains wide.

Although shadows were creeping up the hillside, there was still some sun up high on the foothills. The clump of aspen that sat at the upper edge of one canyon was yellowed, and the leaves on the scrub oak were dried brown. The sky was hazed a soft red.

Manuela seldom looked out this window. Sometimes, she would open the curtains to let in the morning sun, but even then she would prepare her meals, or sweep the floor, or wash her dishes and not once glance up the hill at her grandfather's house. She'd kept the curtains open when Will was here, when she knew he was coming, knowing that he might find it uncomfortable to be shut inside such a small space with an old woman he didn't know. She had looked up hill at the old house for a little while that first day Will had worked, and earlier today when he'd gone up there with that Griego man. But almost always she avoided looking at it, and she had almost laughed out loud at Will when he mentioned tearing it down. As if that was what she wanted. As if what she wished for so close to death was a better view of the foothills.

The house sat still and quiet now up the slope. The pile of trash at the south end of it was bigger than she'd thought it would be. She could see the old oak table where her grandfather had eaten his meals, the coiled spring from the bed where he'd slept. She could picture the three rooms with their slanted dirt floors and their swelled walls swept clean and empty. Each one of them leading to another. And as she and the boy stood gazing out the window, the far north window of the old house suddenly closed, as if someone inside had pulled it shut. And then, beyond the house, one of the ropes hanging from piñon tree began to sway.

Manuela García moaned softly and lowered her eyes. In the near dark of her kitchen, she felt as if what was in her grandfather's house might make its way down the hill into her own house. And what she would do then she didn't know. What she did know, though, was that the overwhelming sadness of it would be too much for her to bear.

She raised her head and picked up the small figure made of wood. She touched her lips against the top of the boy's head and looked again out the window. "There is no wind," she whispered. "Did you see?" And then from the window in the middle room came a flutter of fabric from the cloth that hung from a nail on the window frame. It billowed out, as if suddenly taken by a breeze and then, just as quickly, fell still.

"Callete, mi hijo," Manuela said, softly. "He'll come back. You'll see. In just a little while, he'll come back to us."

# SEVEN

⚜AFTER LEAVING FELIPE, Will drove straight home. It wasn't much after noon, and he figured with the kids in school and it being Estrella's day to check on her grandmother, he'd have a few hours to himself. He parked his truck and got out and went inside. He ate a quick lunch and then made a pot of coffee and took it and a cup out to the woodpile off to the side of the house. He'd hauled a couple of loads of spruce and pine out of the mountains earlier that month, and there was still the raw odor of cut wood mixed with sawdust and chainsaw oil. He rolled a block onto a flat end and sat down. Then he poured a cup of coffee, crossed his legs, and lit up a cigarette.

It was warm in the sun, and he was glad he'd decided to come home. He knew that if he'd returned to the old García house, he would have spent the afternoon killing time, not really sure what to do. He took a sip of coffee and watched a hawk soar far overhead. It hovered still for a moment and then tilted its wings and swooped down so low over the foothills that Will lost sight of it. He took another hit off his cigarette, and it struck him that Felipe was right. Whatever was in the wall of the old García house was Manuela's problem and if he'd had any sense, instead of dragging Felipe all the way up there, he should have just told the old woman what he thought he'd found and let her figure it out. Felipe's words came back to him.

"It's probably her relative up there. Who else could it be?"

Will stood up, stepped out his cigarette, and picked up the axe. Tomorrow, he thought. First thing tomorrow, I'll talk to her about this.

He was working his way through the pile, splitting wood and stacking it against the side of the house, and hadn't gotten all that far when Estrella came driving up the road.

"What are you doing here?" she called out through the open window. She parked next to Will's pickup and got out of her truck, a grin on her face. "I'm so glad to see you," she said.

"I'm glad to see you, too," Will said, and once again, it surprised him that that was true. He set the axe in the chopping block and straightened up slowly. The muscles in his back were already sore and tight.

"Why are you home so early?" Estrella asked, walking over. She rose up on her toes and kissed him. "You smell like wood," she said.

"I knocked off early. I ran into something I didn't expect and decided to get out of there."

"So you came home to chop wood."

"Yes," Will said. "I came home to chop wood."

"I'm glad," she said, "because I didn't have such a good time today."

"What happened?"

Estrella rolled her eyes and shook her head. "I don't want to talk about it now. We have an hour before the girls get home." She took the sleeve of Will's shirt and pulled a little. "Come on, Will," she said.

Inside, the house was cool, and Estrella was out of her clothes and under the blanket before Will had his boots off.

"I was at Nana's house," Estrella said, looking over at Will who was bent over undoing the laces of his boots. "If you wouldn't tie them in knots," she said, "they would come off faster."

"I know that," Will said.

She leaned toward him and ran her fingers down his back and then lay back down. She ran her hands over her breasts and down her belly, and then folded them together and stared at the ceiling. "When I got there," she went on, "the front door was wide open, and I couldn't find her anywhere. At first, I thought that maybe Monica had taken her somewhere. You know how she likes to go to the cafe sometimes and complain to Pepe about his burritos. But then I remembered that Monica said she was going to Las Sombras early early, and besides, Nana would never have left the door wide open like that. You know how she is about keeping those ants out."

Will tossed his boots away from the bed and pulled off his socks. "I take it you found her," he said. "Where was she?"

"She was over by the ditch," Estrella said. "Standing under that big tree."

"The one the owl was in?"

"No, not that one. That was the apple tree. She was under that big one. The cottonwood with all those dead branches. Now stop talking and listen to my story. At first, I was so happy to find her that that was all I could think. You don't know, Will. I felt like I'd lost one of our girls." And here, she paused for a few seconds. "Well, no, that's not true, but it was a little like that." She glanced over at Will who had his shirt off and was unbuttoning his pants. She breathed out a soft humming sound and then turned her head and looked up again at the ceiling. She took in a deep breath and let it out slowly.

"I don't even know how I saw her," Estrella said. "I was on my way to the neighbors' when I just caught sight of her out of the corner of my eye."

Estrella was half walking, half running to the neighbors' when she saw her grandmother standing in the shade of the cottonwood tree that grew near the edge of the ditch. The old woman was wearing a dress that hung loose below her knees with a thin, torn sweater over it. Her hands were wrapped around her like she was freezing cold. For a second, Estrella just stared, and then she hurried over to her. "Nana," she said, a little out of breath. "What are you doing here? You had me so worried." The old woman was staring straight ahead. Her face was paler than usual, and there were bits of dried leaves in her hair. Estrella stepped in front of her and put her hands on her grandmother's arms. "Nana," she said again. "Come, let's go home and get cleaned up."

"I would climb this tree with my sister when we were little girls," the old woman said, the words coming out of her mouth in a rush. "Did you know that?" Her arms were still wrapped around her body and her head was trembling slightly. "We would sit in the branches with a burlap bag full of stones and wait for those Montoya and Ortiz boys to walk by. And when they did, we would throw stones at them until they ran away. Once, I hit Flavio Montoya in the ear and he left crying like a little baby. But those Montoyas were always like that, crying over every little thing."

"Nana," Estrella said, yet again, and then she fell quiet. The grandmother she knew was brusque and sharp-tongued, and if she had something to say it was usually about how her granddaughters could never do one thing right and that the neighbors were even worse. Never had Estrella heard her speak of her childhood, let alone of climbing trees with her sister and throwing rocks at boys. She watched as the old woman finally dropped her arms and looked at her.

"You're not Monica, are you?" the old woman said.

"No," Estrella said. "I'm Estrella."

"Of all my grandchildren, Monica is my favorite."

"I know," Estrella said, although she didn't and would never know why.

"Let me tell you some things for your book," the old woman said. "Oh sí, maybe I'm old, but I still remember. My tío Selfino was my mother's brother and he lived down in the llano. The house is gone now. It burned one winter night when the stove was so hot it caught the vigas on fire. But even now, if you look close in the sagebrush, you can find small piles of rocks and mud and charred pieces of wood where the house stood. Every year, by himself, my tío Selfino would plaster the outside of the church so that the walls did not wash away from the winter snows. He would do this in the autumn when the rains were gone and the days were still warm. And when he was done, the men would bring their whiskey, and the women would bring pots and platters of food, and the walls of the church would still be damp with mud and straw, and it would look like it had grown out of the earth.

"My tío Selfino was married to a woman, Reycita was her name, who was not from here. She was older than her husband and seldom left her house. She died when their house burned, and those who found her said she was like a blackened limb from a juniper tree. She and Selfino had two children. They were my first cousins, and both were boys. When I was young, they would come to my house when they were sure no one was there but me. One, Eliseo, was a little older than I was. He never married and died of a bad heart thirty years ago. The other was named Frutoso. He was older and was killed by one of his own sons a long time ago, and why one of his sons would hit him with an axe, no one ever asked. The two of them would come to my house and make me take off all of my clothes. My chest then was like a boy's. And when I said no, Frutoso would push against me. He was big, even as a boy, and he would say that if I didn't, he would tell his father that I had, but if I did, he would never speak a word. That he just wanted to see. But you know, hija, how that goes.

"They would make me lie down on my back. I would keep my legs and my eyes closed tight, and they took turns lying on top of me. When my father found out about this, he talked to both my tío Selfino and his wife. I don't know what they told him. I only know that when he came home, he called me a name I did not know and beat me. My mother said nothing. She kept quiet and stayed in the kitchen cooking with my sister. I still can remember the meal we ate that night. It was beans and posole, and the tortillas my mother kept between two towels were still warm."

And here, Nana wrapped her arms around her body again, and hugged herself. She looked past her granddaughter, looked out at what had once been an alfalfa field and beyond that, the low-lying foothills to the west.

"You should put that in your book, hija," the old woman said. "It is another story of our family that I remember."

Estrella was lying in the crook of Will's arm, her head on his shoulder. She could feel the length of his body, his skin cool against hers. She could smell sweat and wood and could feel the callouses on his hand scratch lightly along her arm.

"So," she said. "I'm telling you that."

Will grunted softly, not quite sure what to say. He felt as though it would be easy to say the wrong thing. He took in a deep breath and let it out slowly. "I'm sorry that happened to her," he said.

For a few seconds, Estrella was quiet. And then she asked, "Do you ever think of leaving here, Will?"

"Leaving where?"

"Leaving here," Estrella said. "This village. What is it that holds you here?"

"You," Will said.

"No," Estrella said. "I know that. But you were here before me. Other than me and the girls, you have no family holding you. Tell me why you stayed here."

There had been times in the past when he'd thought of leaving Guadalupe. Times when he'd had enough of living in a place where nothing seemed to make sense, from the people to the weather. Times when he'd been left to himself for too long or been given a hard time or been out of work for months, and he'd wondered why he didn't just throw his stuff in the bed of his pickup and go somewhere where things might be easier. But he hadn't. In fact, he'd never really been close to leaving. He'd been rooted to this place from the first moment he'd seen it.

He'd been driving south when his truck broke down on an empty stretch of highway. He'd walked miles until he finally came to the upper edge of this valley. It had been close to sunset, and stretched out below him he could see fields of alfalfa and old adobes and ditches that ran everywhere. Mountains surrounded it on all sides, and aspen trees ran along the three creeks. The air was tinged red and smelled of smoke, and there was the sense that this village had been here forever. Before he had even stepped foot into the valley he knew he might never leave it. And he didn't quite know how to put that into words.

"I don't know, Estrella," he said, staring up at the ceiling. "I just kind of fell into this place. And now, I can't see myself anywhere else." He ran his hand down her arm. "Could you leave?"

Estrella grunted softly. She shifted her weight and turned onto her side. She ran her hand across his chest and down to his belly. "I don't know, either," she said. "I think before yesterday, it wasn't even a thought. But after hearing Nana's stories, I realized that much of what I believe might be wrong. And then, listening to her today, it all just made me sad. It made me feel like there are two villages here, and I only knew the one I wanted to see."

"Maybe every place is like that," Will said.

"Maybe," Estrella said. "Maybe you're right. But in a different place I wouldn't care." She slid up a little higher and looked down at him. "But I know one thing," she said. "I know I could never leave you." Then she kissed him. She smiled against his mouth and took his lip in her teeth and bit down gently. She slung her leg across his waist and felt him stir against her thigh. She closed her eyes and, again, a soft sound came from her mouth.

I make that happen, she thought. I am the one who makes him like that, and no one else ever will. And then she let her weight fall against him, and her hand pulled at his hair bringing him as close to her as she could.

Telesfor Ruiz's house wasn't far from Will's. It hadn't been in the best of shape when the old man had lived there thirty years before, but over the years a dull, sunken look had settled over it. Some of the tin on the roof had pulled loose, and the front portal where Will had sometimes sat with the old man was sagging badly. The plywood nailed over the doors and windows was clouded black and some of the edges had warped loose from the frames. Like Manuela García's grandfather's house, the land around it was overrun with sagebrush and weeds. It was where Will and his daughters always stopped for a little while at the end of their walk along the base of the foothills. The girls were not allowed to go there by themselves.

"Anything can happen in an old, empty house," their mother had told them. "There are rats there and spiders and bats and snakes nesting in the walls." And other things as well, she thought, but didn't say. "You are never to go there without me or your father. Do you understand?" And more often than not it was Ella that Estrella would stare at. It wasn't so much that she didn't trust her oldest daughter, but she knew there was a lot of Will in her. The part that could sometimes drift away in her mind to a place where Estrella couldn't follow. And when that happened, she didn't want it to be around some old, empty adobe that should have been torn down long ago.

As soon as they came close to Telesfor Ruiz's house, Emilia would run ahead. She would walk around the place and look inside through the cracks around the doors and windows. She would peer in at the table that still stood in the shadows of one room, and the dulled curtains that hung just behind the warped plywood, and the cup and one bowl that stood beside the sink. She would stare and wonder what this house was like when it wasn't old, who had sat at the table, if there had been cereal in the bowl, and if children had ever lived here. And if they had, had they ridden a donkey to school through the snow in the winter, if there were even schools way back then.

Ella would follow along more slowly, kicking at the loose dirt for things to find. Once, she had found a rusted axe head, the mouth of it split wide open. Another time, she had found a flat bottle full of dead bugs, the neck plugged with dirt. This she put in the cigar box she kept on the table beside her bed, along with the other things she had found. Pot shards, flakes of obsidian, a torn page from her favorite book, a mouse skull that was missing its front teeth, a photograph of her mother as a little girl, the handle from a coffee cup that had belonged to her grandmother, sun-stained pieces of old glass, a chewed carpenter's pencil, a one-legged ballerina from a music box, five black buttons from the shirt her father had been wearing the day he fell off a roof, and a picture of him and Felipe that had been taken twenty-five years before. They were both grinning in this photograph and holding beers. Behind them were the sunlit foothills and the pickup Will had once owned. Her father was shirtless, his chest smooth and burnt brown, and he was so skinny. He was smiling in a way that made her think he had just said something funny, and she would try to guess just what it was he might have said to Felipe. There was not one bit of gray in his hair, and at night, before sleep, she would wonder what it would be like to have a father so young.

Now, she was sitting beside Will on a half-rotted log near where Telesfor Ruiz had kept his wood pile. The ground around them was black from decades of bark and wood chips. She watched Emilia walk to the far edge of the house and disappear around behind it, and she wondered what would happen if her sister was never seen again. She wondered what her father would do, if her mother would cry. She wondered if she would even miss her sister, and what it would be like to have a room all to herself. She leaned her head against Will's arm and stared at the boarded-up windows and the torn up roof. She tried to picture her father inside drinking coffee with the old man who had lived there.

"Papa," she said. "What about the time Telesfor brought you that sheep head?"

"What about it?" Will said. He, too, was gazing at the old house and figured he'd give Emilia a couple of minutes before he yelled at her to come back.

"Tell me about it."

Will looked down at his oldest daughter. "Aren't you sick of that story?"

"No," Ella said. She could smell sweat and tobacco on her father's shirt. She picked at a piece of straw stuck in the cloth. "It's different every time you tell it," she said.

"Is it?" Will said. It occurred to him that if Ella was right, it was possible that not even he knew what was true in his own life. He sat up a little straighter and shifted his arm around Ella's shoulders. From behind the house he could hear Emilia beating on something with a stick.

"Yes," his daughter said. "It's always different."

"All right," he said, thinking that at least she'd picked a story that was short. "I'll tell it, and you can tell me if it's changed." He blew out a slow breath.

"It was the first winter I was here," he said, "and I knew no one."

One day in early November, Will told his daughter, a storm came into the valley. Earlier that day, it had been warm, so warm that Will had spent it splitting wood and stacking it against the side of the house in only a light shirt. But by mid-afternoon a bank of dark clouds could be seen far to the west, and the sky overhead was streaked a dull white. Just before dark, the wind picked up, the temperature dropped, and it began to snow. Will didn't think much of it at the time, but by morning two feet of snow lay on the ground and the air was gray with clouds.

It snowed for six straight days. The mountains were buried in low hanging clouds, and what road there was was gone. Snow drifted high against the walls of the house. The vigas in the ceiling creaked with the weight of it. Gusts of wind tore at the stovepipe and battered the windows. Will didn't know what to think. He had come from a place where, even if the winters were brutal, they at least had the decency not to begin until December. It wasn't like this, where one moment everything was still and quiet, and the next the wind was howling through the cracks around the door and the air you breathed was full of snow.

Just before dark on the third day of the storm, Will heard a pounding on his door. When he opened it, a gust of wind bit into his face and snow spilled into the room. Standing just outside was Telesfor Ruiz. Behind him, all Will could see was the shadow of trees. The old man was dressed in layers of coats and irrigation boots. His face was burnt from the cold, and beads of ice cornered his mouth and eyes. A wool cap was pulled over his head, and in one hand he held a burlap sack. He told Will that the storm would be here for days and that he had brought him a few things. He said that he did not wish to sit in his house by the fire and think about his neighbor, who was new to this place and knew nothing, slowly starving to death. When Will asked him to come in, Telesfor tossed the bag onto the floor and shook his head. He said that the wind would blow even harder in a little while, and though he knew the way home even he might get lost in such a storm.

Will watched him walk away from his house. The old man moved slowly, the snow nearly to his waist, his shoulders hunched, the wind blowing hard against his body. When he passed from sight, Will closed the door and brought the bag to the table. When he opened it, he found six stale tortillas, three cans of small, red hot dogs, a coffee can half full of lard, and the skinned heads of three sheep.

"The last time," Ella said, "you said it was two sheep heads, not three, and there weren't any hot dogs. And you said the storm came in the spring."

"Did I?" Will said, looking at her.

"Yes," Ella said. "You said it was spring, and you thought the seasons were going backwards. And you said he brought you donuts. Not tortillas."

Will shook his head. "I don't remember saying that," he said.

"I do," Ella said. "You even told me that you wanted to walk him home, but Telesfor knew you'd get lost so he didn't want you to. If it was me, I would have gone to his house and stayed there. Then I would have someone to talk to."

Will smiled. "I didn't think of doing that," he said. "Maybe you should tell the story next time."

"Oh, papa," Ella said. She slapped his leg gently and felt something hard in his pocket. She put her fingers around it. "What's this?" she asked.

Will shifted his body, slid his hand in his pocket, and brought out the marble he'd found in the middle room of the old García house. He'd forgotten he had it. He tossed it up and down a few times, and then held it out on the palm of his hand. "What's it look like?" he said.

"It looks like a marble," Ella said. She could see that it was white and marked with gray, and that there was a chip on one side. She thought it must have been a boy's. She reached out and took it from her father's hand. "Can I have it?" she asked.

A slight feeling of unease went through Will and, just as fast as it had come, it was gone. He watched as Ella held the marble between her thumb and index finger as if to shoot it. It was a bit too big for her fingers. "Yeah," he said. "I guess you can have it." He looked over at the house and then pushed up to his feet. "Emilia!" he called out.

"What?" And her voice sounded small and far away.

"Let's go. It's time to go home."

And a moment later, the three of them walked back through the sagebrush to Estrella.

That night, after the kitchen had been cleaned and the house straightened up, after Ella and Emilia had gone to bed, Estrella was at the table making lunches for her daughter to take to school the next day, and Will was sitting near the open door, smoking. He could feel the chill from outside on his face. It had been a long day, and he was tired. He took a hit off his cigarette and blew the smoke out the open door. He watched Estrella wrap the sandwiches and stick them in two paper bags. Then she picked up an apple and a pear.

"Which one?" she said, looking at Will.

"The apple," he said. "The pear will turn brown and Emilia will throw it away."

Estrella smiled a little. "She will, won't she?" she said. She put one of each in the two paper bags and folded the tops. "There," she said.

"Estrella," Will said.

"Yes?" she said, looking at him again.

Will took one last hit off his cigarette, stubbed it out on the sole of his boot and tossed it out the open door. Then he looked back at her. "This job I'm working on," he said. "For Manuela García? In one of the walls of the house I found some bones. I think they're the bones of a child."

The image of her grandmother as a little girl alone in her house with her two older cousins had been in Estrella's mind nearly all afternoon and evening. Making love with Will and listening to her daughters go on about one thing or another at dinner had helped chase it away for a while, but even then it had never been far from her thoughts. And every time it pushed to the front of her mind, it wasn't Nana's face she saw lying rigid beneath Frutoso, but Ella's or Emilia's. It made her afraid for her daughters. It made her feel as if nothing in the world was safe, and that not only was there nothing she could do about that, but her daughters could be hurt horribly by someone for absolutely no reason at all other than that they were little girls. She was going to tell Will all this in bed. Until now. Now, she felt as if Will had burrowed into her mind and dug out something even worse.

"What?" she said.

"It seems," Will said, "that I've found the bones of some kid buried in the house I'm working on. And I'm not sure what to do about that." And then he went on to tell her everything that had happened from the moment he'd walked into the old García house up to hauling Felipe over there that morning. When he was done, he was smoking yet another cigarette and Estrella was sitting in a chair in front of him. She was leaning forward and had listened without saying a word.

"Maybe Felipe's wrong," she said, finally.

"No," Will said, smiling a little. "He's not wrong."

"What did he say?"

Will shrugged his shoulders. "He thought I should tell Manuela, that it's got to be her relative in there. He thought I could just plaster over them and forget all about it. He thought that maybe the kid had died in the winter, and instead of waiting until spring to bury him they just stuck him in the wall. You know Felipe. Whatever comes into his head comes out his mouth."

"Yes," Estrella said. "I know Felipe." But even then, she thought, that didn't mean what Felipe had said was wrong. She looked outside. At the darkness just beyond the house, at the cigarette smoke drifting out the doorway. She looked back at Will.

"Did you tell her?" she asked.

"No," he said. "I'm going to in the morning. I took Felipe home and came back here. And you know what happened after that." He smiled, again. For some reason, he could feel the weight of the García house lifting. He didn't know if it was the memory of what he and Estrella had done in bed that afternoon or if just telling her had eased it. "Anyway," he said.

Estrella suddenly sat straight up. "I know what we'll do," she said. "In the morning, you tell Manuela about what you've found, and I'll ask Nana." Then she stood up, leaned over Will, and gave him a quick kiss. She dragged her chair back to the table.

"Ask her what?" Will said.

"I'll just ask her," Estrella said. "She and Manuela are about the same age. They must have been girls together."

"I thought you didn't want to hear any more of her stories," Will said.

"I didn't say that. I said they make me sad." She put the two lunch bags in the refrigerator and looked back at Will. "At least this story is about some other family, not mine." Then she smiled. "There," she said. "Now we have a plan. Come on, Will, let's go to bed."

Sometime in the night, Will woke up suddenly. One minute he was in a deep sleep, and the next his eyes were wide open and he was awake. The house was quiet and still. Estrella was breathing softly beside him, her face turned away, the pillow a mess of dark hair. Out the window, he could see a smattering of stars and the darker shadow of trees over by the creek. He didn't know why he'd woken, but he remembered hearing a sudden sound, like that of a door closing or maybe the metal latch of a window snapping shut. He lay there listening for a moment longer and then slid out from beneath the blankets and left the room.

Ella and Emilia slept with their bedroom door open, and Will had the sick feeling that when he looked inside one of them would be gone. He felt for the light switch on the wall and flicked it on long enough for Ella to sit straight up and Emilia to let out a moan and pull the blankets over her head.

"What?" Ella mumbled.

"Nothing," Will said, softly. "I was just checking. Go back to sleep." And when he switched off the light he heard the rustle

118

of Ella lying back down. He stood there for a moment longer, and then went to the front door and stepped outside.

The air was cool on his skin, and off to the east there wasn't even a glimpse of dawn. The two trucks sat where they'd been parked, and nothing was moving on the road. From far off, he could just catch the faint sound of a trucker downshifting to take the hill out of town.

"Everything's fine," he said to himself. But still a slight edge of uneasiness went through him, as if he'd forgotten something important. He shook his head, suddenly aware that he was outside naked in the middle of the dark looking for something that was never there.

# EIGHT

❋ **WHEN BERNABE MEDINA WOKE** just before dawn, he lay in bed for a moment and then, half asleep, reached out a hand and felt for his wife. He did this every morning, and like every other morning for the past three years all his outstretched hand felt was the cool, smooth expanse of the sheet.

"Pelimora," he said, as he said each morning in the darkness of his bedroom. "Where did you go?"

Even after three years, and even after finding himself alone in his bed each morning, he still expected to see his wife in the kitchen when he went to make his coffee. He expected to see her sitting at the table sipping from her own cup, her legs crossed, her hair not yet brushed, smiling a little as he came into the room. Whenever he was gone from the house, he pictured her writing the poems that she would read to him later, or straightening up the house from the day before, or pulling weeds from among the flowers that grew along the front of the house, all the time listening for the sound of his truck. When he sat in the living room staring out the window or at nothing on the television, he waited to hear the sounds she would make while cooking, the scraping of a ladle, water boiling in a pot, the rasp of corn husks, the soft hum her voice sometimes made. Even after her death three years before, a part of him believed that Pelimora was just in the next room. But when he went to look for her, she was always gone, just beyond his reach.

They had been married for sixty-seven years, and though he was often irritated with having to hear yet one more poem about a sad sunset or how one's heart could beat like a soft rainfall or why she persisted in planting flowers around the house instead of cucumbers, he felt her absence in every waking moment. Other than his sheep and maybe his pickup, which had had the decency to start even on the coldest morning for the past twenty-five years, Pelimora had been the only good thing in his life.

They had been seventeen years old when they married, and so shy and timid that they had slept in their clothes on their wedding night. Early the next morning, Bernabe had woken to the touch of his young wife's hand on his back. He had turned away from her sometime in the night, and for a moment he just lay there staring at the wall beside the bed and feeling Pelimora's hand move beneath his shirt. Then he turned to face her.

"Pelimora," he said.

"I don't want to begin our marriage this way, Bernabe," she said. Her eyes were damp, as if she'd been crying while he slept.

"What way?"

"Like this," she said, and her fingers pulled at the neck of his shirt. "I want to see what's beneath this. My mother told me that when I married, the man I chose would be mine to do with as I wished," and here she pulled again at his shirt. "I chose you, and I don't wish this."

Bernabe opened his mouth to speak, and then was smart enough to remain quiet. His own mother had never said one thing to him about marriage other than that she had had enough of boys and preferred only granddaughters. And his father, over a bottle of whiskey, had shaken his head and said that women had no respect for a man who did not show them a thing or two now and then, and Bernabe should never forget that. When he'd seen his two older brothers a few days before the wedding, all they'd done was grin and tell him that all he now had to look forward to was one bad time after another. That even the one good thing a wife was good for was only good for a little while.

"I have some dreams, Bernabe," Pelimora said, unbuttoning his shirt. She could see his bare chest now, and she ran her hands over it down to his belly. Then she looked up at him and smiled.

"Pelimora," Bernabe said, his voice choked. And though he didn't know it at the time, it was at that moment that his life turned away from that of his brothers and went the way of his seventeen-year-old wife.

Now Bernabe got out of bed slowly and dressed in the dark in the same clothes he'd worn the day before. He walked through the house to the kitchen, glancing at the table in the center of the room. He went to the stove, put on a pot of coffee, and then went to the window and looked out.

He could see his sheep huddled quietly in their pen. It was still too early for them to call for him. There was a time when he didn't have to pen them up at night, a time when they could spend their nights out in the field. There was always the stray coyote that might bother his lambs, but nothing like the packs of dogs that now roamed the village like they thought it was theirs. It seemed that no matter how many of them he shot, there were more of them the next day. He wondered just where in hell they were all coming from. He thought they were like those hordes of Mongols he'd seen on a television program a long time ago. No matter how many of them fell dead, there were still more that wanted to invade his field and hurt his sheep, who never bothered anyone.

The water was boiling now, and he could smell the strong odor of coffee. He shut off the stove, poured a cup, and went back to the window. It was beginning to get light, the sky above the foothills a dull, pale white. Bernabe looked down the road that led to Manuela García's place. Her house was just a half mile away past a couple of untended alfalfa fields. There was enough light now for him to see how the road curved sharply into her drive and the large cottonwood trees that shielded the house from sight.

Not for the first time, Bernabe wondered what that old woman who lived there was doing. What it had been like for her to have lived so much of her life alone in a house at the far edge of the village. In all the decades they had been neighbors, Bernabe had been to her house only once.

It had been just after the death of Manuela García's grandfather. Ray Pacheco, who was the Guadalupe police officer back then, and Tomás Cortez had found the old man hanging from a piñon tree in the woods not far from where one of the creeks spilled into the valley. It was early October when they found him, and they'd been hunting elk.

"I don't know where his boots went to," Tomás later told Bernabe, "but he was barefoot and his feet were all swelled up like they'd filled with blood. He'd been beaten around the face, and both his hands were broken. His fingers were all twisted, and one hand was bent backwards. I didn't even know who the hell he was until Ray told me it was Bolivar García. Even then I wasn't sure who he meant. Just having heard things here and there about him. I couldn't figure out how a man in that shape could manage to hang himself, but I wasn't about to argue with Ray. You know how he gets. Everything's nice and easy if you see things his way."

Here, Tomás Cortez shook his head. "So," he said, "Ray, he cuts him down, and then stands looking at him like the old man is an elk he'd just shot. Then he tells me to go back to the village and get Daniel Lucero and Telesfor Ruiz to help bury him. When I asked about the priest and mention that it might be a good idea to tell his family, Ray stares at me for a long time. He tells me that this old man never once went to church and that all the family he has is a granddaughter, and that he knows for a fact she could care less about what we do with him. And if she does, then he'll go talk to her later. He tells me not to forget to bring a couple of shovels and a pick, and that I better get going or we'd end up stuck out there in the dark burying him."

"I don't know," Tomás went on, scratching the side of his face. "Don't tell nobody I said this, but it was like Ray knew we were going to find him out there. Like he knew all along. And I'll tell you one more thing, next time Ray Pacheco asks me to go elk hunting with him, I'm going to tell him I'm too busy to hunt elk anymore."

A week or so after Bolivar García's death, Pelimora cooked a platter of enchiladas and asked Bernabe to take them to Manuela García. When he hesitated, she said it was the least they could do, and since she did not care to be near the woman, she thought it would be better if Bernabe were to go.

"We don't even know the woman, Pelimora. How can you say that you don't care for her?"

The kitchen was warm that day and full of the scent of garlic and cilantro and green chili. "She only knows men, Bernabe," Pelimora said, smiling a little. "She will not accept this from me. Please don't ask any more questions. Tell her to keep the platter, that I don't need it to be returned. And you come home quickly."

It was raining as Bernabe walked down the road to Manuela García's house. Not one of those hard, driving rains that sometimes swept into the valley, but a soft, steady drizzle. Clouds draped the foothills. The air was still, and Bernabe could see his breath. He held the platter of food close to his chest, his head dipped so that the rain would not fall on what he was bringing to his neighbor.

The first thing Bernabe noticed when he neared the house was that the curtains were drawn and there was no smoke coming from the stovepipe. The next was that though the house was in decent shape, there was an empty, neglected feel about the place. Dead leaves and branches from the cottonwood trees were lying everywhere. The grass that had grown high over the summer hadn't been cut but had been left to grow wild and now lay beaten down by the rain. Weeds grew up against the side of the house, and off to one side was a pile of firewood mixed with old warped boards and rolls of tar paper and rusted rims from a wagon and a warming over from a cookstove and a few splintered wood barrels that might have held whiskey and the rotting skull and hide from the carcass of a cow. The smell of it was in the air, and Bernabe moved the platter of food to the far side of his body as if afraid the stench might leak into it.

There was no answer when Bernabe knocked on the door. He stood there for a moment not sure what to do. Rain from the eave dripped on his cap, and a trickle of cold water ran down his back. He looked back down the rutted drive at the wet grass and the sodden, yellowed leaves that still hung on the cottonwoods. Then he turned toward the foothill. And that was when he first caught sight of the old García house. He grunted and pulled back his head.

"What is that?" he said, out loud. He'd lived his whole life in the village and couldn't imagine how he hadn't known this was here.

It was a long one-story adobe with a pitched roof. There were three windows facing him that he thought must open into separate rooms. Other than some cracks in the plaster around the windows, a torn sheet of metal on the roof, the house seemed to be in pretty good shape. Just a little ways above the house and off to the south was a tall piñon tree. It stood by itself in the midst of the sagebrush, and hanging down from an upper limb was a rope swing. Just as Bernabe began to wonder not only where this house had come from but why on earth someone had bothered to build it where there was no water, no road, and no pasture, he caught sight of Manuela García.

She was standing motionless just outside the door on the south side of the house. So still that Bernabe hadn't noticed her before. She was wearing a black dress, and even from so far away Bernabe could see that, with the rain, it was plastered tight against her body. Her arms were bare and bone white. A shiver ran through him, as if he could feel the fabric of the dress wet against his own skin. The door to the house was wide open, and Manuela was leaning forward a little, her shoulders hunched, staring inside.

What is she doing? he thought. What is she looking at? He waited for her either to step inside the house or turn and notice him standing outside her door. The rain kept falling, a slow, steady drizzle. There wasn't a breath of air, and the clouds hung so low that the grayness seemed to bleed into the house up on the slope, into the sagebrush, into the woman standing so still that Bernabe felt he could have been staring at a painting.

He wasn't sure how much longer he stood there watching, but it was long enough for the back of his shirt to grow cold and wet from the dripping water, long enough for the muscles in his arms to ache from holding the platter of enchiladas. He wondered if he should go up there and say something to her, but what that might be he didn't know. And then the light grew a shade darker and Manuela García suddenly shook her head hard. Her body sagged, as if she had been holding her breath all this time. Then she wrapped her arms around her chest and turned and began to walk away from the old house.

When she got to the edge of the slope, she slipped and fell awkwardly. Bernabe could see a flash of white as her dress rose high up her legs. She sat still for a moment and then slowly got to her feet. Her arms hung at her sides now, and the sagebrush grabbed at her dress as she walked down the path.

She's like a blind woman. Bernabe didn't so much think that thought as the words came from outside him and slid into his mind. She was halfway down the hill when she fell again, and Bernabe watched her cradle her knees with her arms, and lower her forehead onto them. The rain had slowed now, and the clouds were beginning to lift. Trails of mist clung to the foothills. Bernabe could feel a deeper chill in the air now, and he could hear Manuela weeping. Above her, the house sat still and quiet. The door to it was closed, and he couldn't remember if she had shut it. Perhaps some breeze he hadn't felt had pulled it closed. He looked at her again as she raised her head and slowly got to her feet. Then, as if embarrassed for watching so long, he put the platter of food down just outside the door to the house, stepped away, and began to make his way back to Pelimora, leaving Manuela García to herself.

That was a long time ago I was at her house, Bernabe thought to himself. He sipped at his coffee. It had grown cold. Que? Maybe fifty years ago. Maybe even more.

It was light outside now, though the sun was still behind the mountains. Bernabe could hear his sheep calling for him. From deeper in the house, he heard a slight rustling, as if Pelimora was straightening the bed. He put his cup in the sink and walked through the kitchen to the front door. He put on the jacket that was hanging from a hook, and went outside to feed his sheep.

# NINE

❀WILL LEFT THE HOUSE EARLY the next morning. He didn't even bother to pack a lunch, figuring that after talking to Manuela García his day would be pretty much done. Ella and Emilia were still asleep when he left, and Estrella was stirring oatmeal into a pot of boiling water. She was wearing one of Will's T-shirts and baggy pajama bottoms. Her feet were bare. When he kissed her goodbye, she lowered the flame on the stove and turned to him.

"You're leaving?"

"Yes."

"But you'll be home early."

"I should be," he said.

"Good. We can talk then. While the girls are still in school. I think I'll go see Nana after I get them on the bus."

"Sounds good," Will said, although he'd almost forgotten about Estrella's plan to talk to her grandmother. In fact, he'd woken up feeling as though he'd made a big deal out of nothing and in a little while all Manuela García would be was some old woman he'd once done a little work for. He ran his hand up Estrella's ribs and cupped her breast. She smiled and leaned into him.

"You be careful, Will."

"I will," he said. Then he kissed her again and left the house.

The lights were on inside Felix's Cafe. A couple of pickups, along with Pepe's small car and Ambrosio's beat-up bike that he never rode anywhere, were parked in front of the place.

Will pulled off the highway and parked beside Pepe's car. Through the plate glass window he could see a group of guys drinking coffee at a table. Pepe was standing beside them. Ambrosio was probably in the kitchen rolling out tortillas or still in his small trailer behind the cafe. Will shut off the engine and got out of the truck. Then, instead of going inside, he leaned back against the closed truck door, lit a cigarette, and looked out over the valley. The village was still and quiet, the colors this early in the morning muted and dulled, and there was, as always, the faint odor of woodsmoke. Will could feel the air cool on his skin. There was a light haze of clouds that he knew would burn off as soon as the sun rose.

Off in the distance, he could see the clump of trees where his house sat. By now, he thought, Estrella would have the girls up. They'd be in the kitchen eating oatmeal, still in their pajamas, too tired to do much more than mumble at whatever their mother asked. Further south, in a direct line across the valley from his own place, Manuela García's house was hidden behind the cottonwood trees. Will wondered what the old woman was doing. Was she still lying in bed or sitting alone in her kitchen, the lights off, waiting for him? He heard the door to the cafe open. Manny Varoz was coming out the door. He stopped when he saw Will.

"Hey, Will," Manny said. He was a younger guy who laid block and poured slabs for foundations. Will had worked now and again with his father, Manuel, years before. The three of them were on the same jobsite one day when Manuel's heart had stopped beating. It had been a cold morning in mid-January when this had happened. The ground had been frozen solid and covered with an inch of hard, crusted snow. Manny had been about fourteen years old then, and Will remembered the boy standing off by himself near a pile of sand and cinder blocks, a fog of frost in the air, staring at his father lying on the ground. Manny and his two older brothers had managed to keep the business going after their father's death. Most of their work was down in Las Sombras.

"Hey, Manny," Will said, smiling a little. He pushed off the truck door and stepped out his cigarette. "Where are you off to?"

"I got to get my brother and check on the cows. Finished up a pretty big job a couple of days ago. How about you?"

Will shrugged. "Just small stuff," he said.

"I thought I saw you with Felipe yesterday," Manny said. "You two working together again?"

"No," Will said. "I just take him for a ride sometimes. Kind of like taking the dog for a walk."

Manny laughed. "You two," he said. "Nothing ever changes." He walked over to his pickup, pulled open the door, and looked back. "Hey," he said. "I heard you and Felipe found some dead body buried in a house. What's the story?"

For a couple of seconds, Will didn't say a word. He didn't know quite what to say. "Where'd you hear that?" he said, finally.

"At the lumberyard. Yesterday. Lloyd was in there telling everyone. He said that if anyone would be running around digging things up, it would be you. But you know how he is."

"Yeah, I know how he is," Will said. Will had been in Guadalupe only a little while when he'd run into Lloyd at a gas station. He'd pulled up next to Will's truck, rolled down his window, and told him to get his ass out of the village, that he wasn't wanted around here. That had happened a long time ago, and even if Will didn't think about it much anymore, he hadn't forgotten.

"So, what's the story?"

"There isn't one, Manny," Will said. "I found some old bones in a house I'm working on. They could have been from anything. Sounds like someone's running with this for fun."

"That's what I thought," Manny said. "But you be careful, bro. You know how people are."

"I will," Will said. He watched the man he remembered as a boy get into his truck. And as Manny drove off, Will wondered just how many people Felipe had told about this.

The inside of the cafe was warm and smelled of old coffee and raw, wet pinto beans. Pepe was still over at the table talking with the three men sitting there. They were all drinking coffee, and one of them stared openly at Will when he walked through the door. But with Manny stuck in his mind, Will wasn't sure if the stare meant something or if he was beginning to imagine things. Felix García, Pepe's father, was sitting by himself in the far corner.

Felix had suffered a stroke years and years before and since then hadn't spoken a word. Pepe got him out of bed every morning, helped him dress, and walked him to the same table in the back of the cafe where he would sit hunched over, his head dipped low and shaking, one hand clutched in his lap, the other tapping softly against the tabletop. Will had heard that Felix had once loved his son, had loved his wife, and had loved coming to his cafe before the village was awake to cook his beans and chili. But the only Felix García Will had ever known was this one. A silent, bent old man, and what went on in his mind was anyone's guess.

"What do you need, Will?" Pepe asked from halfway across the room. He made his way over to where Will was standing.

"I just need a coffee to take with me," Will said.

Pepe went to the back wall, filled a cup with coffee and brought it over. "Just take it," he said. "It's a couple hours old."

"Thanks," Will said. "How's your father doing?"

Pepe shrugged. "The same," he said. He was in his sixties but looked old and worn out. There were smudges under his eyes and a sallow look to his skin. His apron was stained with chili and eggs and who knew what else. "Sometimes I think he's getting better, and then he seems worse. Yesterday, I found him by the front window staring out like he wanted to take a walk. I don't even know how he got there all by himself."

Will glanced over at the old man. Felix's body was bent over on itself, his chin so low it almost touched the table. He was wearing a baseball cap.

"Thanks for asking, though," Pepe went on. "His old friends used to stop by and sit with him, but I don't see much of them anymore."

"Yeah," Will said. He wondered what he would do if Felix was an old friend. Would he sit with the old man, or would he just drive by the cafe and make believe Felix wasn't there? "Well," he said. "I better get going."

As Will turned to leave, Pepe said, "Hey, I almost forgot to tell you. Donald Lucero was looking for you."

Will stopped and looked back. "Why?" he asked. Donald Lucero was the village cop and had been pretty much since Will had first come to Guadalupe.

Pepe shrugged and wiped his hands on his apron. "How should I know? He asked if you'd been in and said he wanted to talk to you. If it makes you feel any better, he said it was no big deal. Then he got a call and took off."

From back in the cafe came the sound of Felix's hand tapping louder on the top of the table. Somehow his hat had fallen off and one arm hung low off the table. He was leaning so far to one side that it looked like he might topple over. The three guys at the table glanced over and then looked away. Pepe let out a long breath, and then turned away from Will.

"I'm coming, Papa," he said to nobody at all. "I'm coming."

Will took the drive slow through the village. After all, he thought, it was still early and there was no hurry. Tito's was closed up and the lumberyard not yet open. He took a couple of sips of his coffee, and then rolled down the window and tossed it out. The breeze blowing in was still cool.

He took the hill down to where the valley flattened out. He drove by Levi's junkyard and old adobes set back in trees and wind-blown trailers, tires up on the roof, and fields overgrown with weeds and the abandoned shell of a gas station that Mario Gonzales had thought was a good idea to build more than forty years ago.

At the south end of the village, Will hung a left on the dirt road that led to Manuela García's place. The houses he drove by were quiet. No one was out in the fields. A couple of dogs chased his truck, biting at the tires, until he eased his vehicle off to one side, forcing them into the ditch. He followed the road as it swung north along the creek, and then, off in the distance, he saw Bernabe Medina standing in the middle of the road in front of his house.

After feeding his sheep and telling them that later, later when he was sure there were no dogs, he would let them out in the field, Bernabe walked slowly down his drive and stood out on the road, his hands in his pockets, staring back at his house and the valley beyond.

Far off to the west, he could see sunlight lying on the tops of the foothills, slowly creeping its way down the slopes. And closer, right in front of him, his own house sat still and shadowed.

The alfalfa fields stretching away from all sides lay barren and fallow. Not even enough alfalfa to keep his few sheep happy. Across the valley, trailers dotted the hillside, and near them sat the old adobes that had been left behind. He saw the old Cortez house that had burned down one winter decades ago, and he remembered that not long after that the entire family had disappeared from the village. He saw old corrals and caved-in outhouses and junked cars and tractors sitting in weeds, and a sad, lonely feeling crept over him.

He remembered a time when things weren't like this. A time when neighbors looked out for neighbors and the lines between families were not so fiercely drawn. Not like now, he thought, when no one much cares about anything or anyone, and if they do it's only to hear bad things that might make them feel a little better about their life.

Bernabe remembered a time when the Sanchez family would give a cow to the church every autumn, and there would be a feast, and the Vigils up north would bring their fiddles, and the sweet scent of rotting apples and manure and cut alfalfa would be in the air. There had been the sound of bawling cows and kid's voices along the irrigation ditches at dusk. There had been baseball games at the old ballfield near the base of the foothills where everyone would drink too much beer and whiskey. Ranchers had baled hay all through the summer, and neighbors cut wood together in the mountains.

When did it all change, Pelimora? Bernabe thought to himself. How could I not have seen it happening? Again, he wondered where she was. Was she in the kitchen washing his coffee cup? Or standing at the window looking out at him? And just as the thought came to him that even villages might grow old and die, he heard Will's truck.

Will slowed down as he neared Bernabe. He didn't know what the old man was doing out on the road so early, but he knew the last thing he wanted to do was bury him under the cloud of dust his truck was kicking up. When he drew up alongside Bernabe, Will came to a stop and rolled down his window. The old man turned toward him, his hands still in the pockets of his jacket.

"Buenos días, Bernabe," Will said, leaning out the window a little. "I don't know if you remember me."

"Oh sí," Bernabe said. "I remember you. You did some work on my house." He looked even older to Will, as if the last three years hadn't been so good. Though he still looked fit, a little on the stocky side, there was a drawn, haggard look to his face, like sleep was hard to come by. His eyes were bloodshot, the skin beneath them dark and swollen.

"Yes," Will said, looking over at the house. "I put the shingles on. Maybe three years ago."

"I remember," Bernabe said, nodding his head slowly. "I remember it was just after I lost my wife. I remember you made a big mess, but you cleaned it all up. And my roof has never leaked."

"That's good," Will said, and smiled. "But it's hard to tell with the rain we're getting."

"It's been dry, all right," the old man said. He looked over at the fields. At the stunted plants and the burned-out weeds. "It wasn't like this once," he said, almost as if to himself. "Once these fields were full and green."

"I know," Will said, but he could tell the old man wasn't listening. "I was here then."

For a few seconds, Bernabe just stared off. Then he said, "This village is dying. I don't know how it happened, but it did." When he looked back at Will he felt something snag at the back of his mind, but he didn't know what it was. "If I was a young man," he said, "I would leave this place. I would go somewhere else."

"Sometimes it's hard to leave," Will said, not knowing quite what to say. "You have to have a place to go."

"Maybe," Bernabe said, softly. "Maybe that's true." Then he looked away again. "I don't know," he said. "I don't know what's true." And suddenly, he realized that not only didn't he know what was true, he didn't know where his life had gone, and that great longing filled him again. He looked at the windows of his house and took a slow step away from Will.

"Well," Will said. "I guess I better get going. I'll see you later, Bernabe." He watched the old man take a few more steps away and then put the truck into gear and drove the last half mile to Manuela García's house.

It wouldn't be until much later, when it was already too late, that Bernabe would remember why it was he had walked out to the road early that morning. He had gone there to wait for Will. Not to talk to him about his roof or the village or his life, but to tell him that he was sorry he had given his name to Manuela García. That if Pelimora had been alive, she would have told Will that Manuela García knew things he would never wish to know and that he should stay away from that place.

# TEN

❧ WHEN WILL FINALLY DROVE UP to Manuela García's house, he half expected to see her, arms crossed, hair tied back, face severe, waiting for him beneath the cottonwood trees by the ditch. But other than a flock of small birds that picked up out of the weeds and swooped off, nothing moved outside her house. He parked off to the side and shut off the truck engine. Then he sat there, staring out the windshield and thinking that it had been one hell of a morning already.

He felt a little shaky and knew it wasn't from skipping breakfast or Pepe's bad coffee. He knew it was because in the last thirty minutes Manny Varoz had warned him to be careful (from what, he didn't know), he'd listened to Pepe go on about his failing father, and then Bernabe Medina, who was standing out in the middle of the road as if waiting for him, had told him that the village was dying and if he was smart he'd go live somewhere else. On top of all that, he could still feel Leonardo Martinez and his twin brother, Benito, ticking away in the back of his mind.

"Jesus Christ," Will muttered. "What's up with all these old men?" He pulled a cigarette out of his pocket, lit it, and blew the smoke out the open window. Then he leaned back in the seat and looked over at Manuela García's house.

The sun was still behind the foothills, and it was dark enough that even with the curtains drawn he could tell the lights were off inside. At first glance, the house seemed to be in decent shape, but the more he stared at it, the more he could see the hairline cracks in the plaster, the swollen shingles on the roof, the paint flaking away from the window frames, and the rotted, blackened boards running along the length of the eaves.

He wondered not only why Manuela had decided to fix up her grandfather's house instead of the one she lived in, but who she'd gotten in the past to work around the place. As he sat there smoking, he realized that he knew almost nothing about her. He didn't know if she'd had a husband or children or what neighbors she visited or if there was anyone who looked in on her now and then. All he knew was what little she had told him. And that had only been about the one thing she'd wanted from him. "I want you to fix my grandfather's house before I die," she'd said, staring across the table at him. "I want it to look the way I remember it as a child. That's what I want from you."

I don't think that's going to happen now, Will thought to himself. I think after this morning, we'll be done with each other. He took one last hit off his cigarette, dropped it out the window, and got out of the truck. He stood outside the pickup and stretched out his back. And then, as he walked toward the house, the only thought that made him feel a little better about his morning was that, although Manuela García was old, at least she wasn't another old man.

The front door was closed and there was a quiet, dead feel about the place, as if the old woman was gone or still asleep inside. Will knocked once, and then again harder. He stood there for a moment and when nothing happened, he turned the doorknob gently. It was locked. He thought of calling out for her, but didn't like the idea of waking her if she was sleeping. After all, she had no idea he wanted to talk to her. All she expected of him was to show up and go to work.

He took in a deep breath and looked up the slope at the old house. He figured he could kill some time going up there and getting his tools. Maybe he'd kick around inside for a little while and then come back down and check on her. So, with one more glance at the closed door, and just as the sun crested the foothill, he began to walk up the hill to the old García house.

The first thing he did when he got up there was get rid of the crosses. The day before, they'd just been overwhelming, but this morning, he didn't like even the feel of them. They made the kitchen feel smaller than it was, and he couldn't imagine what had possessed someone to make so many. It was as if whoever had made them had been looking for something over and over again that they could never find.

And the old woman had said, "I don't want them in there, hijo. Just get rid of them."

Some of them were hooked onto rusted wire, others had a spike driven through them, but the adobe was so eroded that they all pulled loose easily. He didn't bother putting them in the pile of trash outside, but just threw them out the kitchen door, thinking that they could be burned later.

When he was done, the room felt better, cleaner somehow, as if he'd gotten rid of something tainted. Out the open door, the pile he'd made was a jumble of twisted wood, each one tied to another with a piece of thin leather. Will almost wished he'd taken them farther from the house to somewhere where they couldn't be seen. From the far end of the house came the sound of the south door closing gently, and from the middle room Will heard the one window creak, as if moved by a breeze. A dribble of dirt fell from the ceiling and hissed onto the top of the cookstove. And, as if the temperature in the room had suddenly dropped, he felt a hard chill run through him.

He was beginning to feel as if there was more to this house than he could see, as if there was always something just beyond his sight. He bent over, picked up a shard of glass he'd missed two days before, and tossed it out the open door. Then, shaking his head a little, he walked into the middle room.

He went to the window and pushed it all the way open. Down the hill, he could see Manuela's house. The curtains were still drawn over the windows in her kitchen. His truck was parked in the shade beneath the cottonwood tree. He turned around and looked at the wall where he'd found the bones. He'd been in the house long enough now that he could make them out clearly.

"Who are you?" he said out loud. "And how in hell did you get in such a place?" Then, not sure just what he was doing or why, he pulled his hammer and a small chisel out of his toolbag and knelt down in front of the bones. He ran his hand over them, flaking away small pieces of mud. And then, with the chisel, he began to carefully chip away at the adobe wall.

The moment Will began digging into the wall of the old García house, the phone in Felipe's kitchen rang. Felipe was in the bathroom taking a piss when he heard Elena scramble out of bed and leave the bedroom to go answer the phone.

"You watch," he said to himself. "It's probably someone calling about a stupid job or one of my sons wanting one more thing."

The morning, he thought, had started pretty good. It was his wife's day off from work, and not one of his grandchildren had showed up. He and Elena had woken early and had, without a word, proceeded to mess around a little bit, which they hadn't done in so long that Felipe had come to believe it might never happen again. Better yet, once they'd started, he'd found himself responding like he had as a young man. And when Elena had shuddered beneath him, her mouth half open, her eyes somewhere far away, he'd thought to himself, Eee, I'm still pretty good at this. Even being together for so long, I can still make my wife feel this way.

Now, sitting on the edge of the bed pulling on his pants, he was wondering what he would do with the rest of this day when Elena came back into the bedroom. She was wearing one of his old shirts and nothing else. The sight of her bare feet and bare legs, and how the shirt hung loose just below her hips made him wonder if what they had done earlier they might try again. He raised his eyes and gave her a look. Then he saw the expression on her face, and whatever thought he'd had of going back to bed with his wife left him. He watched as she folded her arms across her chest, the shirt inching up even a little higher.

"The phone was for you," she said.

Felipe stood up and zipped his pants. He shook his head. "I hate it when people call so early in the morning," he said. "I hope you told them I'm not working anymore, and if they need someone to call Will." He looked at his wife and smiled. "You know, I think I might take it easy today. Maybe do a little digging in the garden. There's still some more potatoes out there."

"It was Flavio Montoya," Elena said, not hearing one word Felipe had just said, "He wants to talk to you about some child you found buried in a wall that I know nothing about."

For some reason, although his wife had spoken only two seemingly simple sentences, Felipe's mind was having trouble shifting from sex to digging in his garden to what she was now saying. All he could think of to say was, "Flavio Montoya? Qué Flavio Montoya?"

Elena grunted sharply and shook her head. "What do you mean what Flavio Montoya?" she said. "The Flavio Montoya

143

who has lived just down the hill from us forever. The one you help with his cows and talk to over the fence. That Flavio Montoya. There is no other Flavio Montoya in this village that I know of. Besides, we're not talking about Flavio right now. We're talking about why my neighbor knows more about this than I do. Why I have to hear a story like this from him instead of from my husband."

"If we're not talking about Flavio," Felipe said, starting to get a little angry, or at least thinking it might help, "why do you keep mentioning him?"

For what seemed like a long time, the two of them just stared at each other. And then, closing her eyes and in a voice that was both patient and aggravated, Elena spoke the one word she knew would stop her husband from squirming like a trapped animal.

"Felipe," she said.

This is all Will's fault, Felipe thought to himself. If he hadn't come over yesterday none of this would be happening. I would be drinking my coffee outside in the sun with nothing to think about but my potatoes. Instead, here I am fighting with my wife over something that doesn't have one thing to do with me. Then, as if from a distance, as if he had his eyes closed and couldn't see, he heard Elena say, "I don't know how you could not have told me about this. On top of that, I don't understand how Flavio heard about it. What did you do, run down the hill and tell him?"

After Will had dropped him off the day before, Felipe had loaded his two grandchildren into his truck and driven to the lumberyard where he'd gone into the office, sat down on a chair across from Joe Vigil, and said, "You won't believe this, primo." Thirty minutes later, he'd stopped at Eli Ortega's garage thinking a story like this might take his mind off his troubles for a little while and make him feel better.

Felipe and Eli Ortega had grown up together, gone to school together, partied together, and worked together. Other than Rudy Duran, Eli was the guy Felipe and Will would call when they needed someone to do the stuff they didn't want to do. Like carry shingles up on a roof or unload block or dig a trench by hand. Eli was a small, wiry man, a little high strung, with six kids and a wife who never had a good thing to say about anyone, especially Eli. And though Felipe and Eli had always been close friends, you'd never have known it from the way they worked together.

Felipe had a habit of telling Eli to do one thing, and when he was half into it, yelling at him to do something else or grabbing the shovel or the hammer or the drill and saying, "Like this, jodido." And the day would go on pretty much like that, Felipe getting more and more impatient and Eli more jumpy. Once, while Eli was struggling to keep his footing up on a roof, Felipe had suddenly grabbed the man's arm from behind and shouted, "Be careful, hombre, or you'll fall," causing Eli to drop to his knees and start shaking like a cowed dog. When Will had asked Felipe later why he felt it was okay to torture Eli, Felipe had shrugged and said that Eli had always been this way.

About a year ago, Eli, at his wife's insistence, had moved into his garage where he ate canned food and watched his children come and go. And not long after that, he'd gone to Las Sombras to see a doctor about a deep, piercing pain he had in his chest. After a series of tests, the doctor told him, according to Eli, that he couldn't find one thing wrong with him, other than that he had a sad heart. When Eli asked what a sad heart was, the doctor told him it was something that sometimes happened to men who live in garages and are married to women who have no use for them.

And now, Felipe could suddenly picture that jodido Eli, contrary to what he promised, running into the house as soon as he left and telling his wife the story who would then tell her sister who would then tell both her husbands, the one who lived with her and the one she thought no one knew about, who, knowing them, told everyone at work at the mine. And who knew how many people Joe Vigil told. He just hoped it wasn't Lloyd Romero, who would pass it on to everyone, even people he didn't know.

Felipe could suddenly picture his one little conversation with Joe and Eli going through the village like a leaf dropped in one of the ditches that ran from the foothills. It would float from field to field, from house to house, until everyone had seen it pass by. And then, wanting to rid himself of that image, he wished all eight of his grandchildren would come running into his house so that he could think about nothing. He let out a long sigh.

"Well," he said.

"Well what?" Elena said.

"I was going to tell you," Felipe said, which wasn't quite true. In truth, he hadn't given it much thought at all. "But with one thing or another. And then I forgot, and when I remembered, I didn't think it was such a big deal."

"You didn't think finding a child buried in the wall of an old house was a big deal? Or you didn't think not telling me was a big deal?"

"Neither," Felipe said. "Both."

Elena closed her eyes and shook her head slowly. She breathed out a soft sound and let her arms fall to her sides. "I didn't tell you this before," she said softly, looking at Felipe, "but you were so good in bed." And when the look on Felipe's face softened and she saw his eyes move down to her legs, she said, "But not so good that I'm going to forget about this. Come. I put coffee on. You can tell me the story that you should have told me yesterday."

"And that's all I know about this," Felipe said to his wife. They were sitting at the table in the kitchen. The door that led outside was open. From where he sat, Felipe could see that it was going to be another warm day full of sun. He could hear birds and, now and again, the bawl of one of Flavio Montoya's cows from far down the hill.

He'd told Elena pretty much everything that had happened the day before, only leaving out a couple of things. He hadn't told her about Manuela García more or less chasing him off her property. It hadn't bothered him so much at the time, but now, sitting across from his wife, he didn't want her to know that a frail, old woman had treated him that way. He'd also skipped telling her that he'd told Eli Ortega the story. Elena had never much cared for Eli and liked his wife even less.

Felipe took a sip of coffee, and then put the cup back down on the table. He stretched out his legs so that his feet were in the sun and folded his hands over his belly. There, he thought, I've fixed this.

Elena had listened to Felipe's entire story without once interrupting. A few things had occurred to her, though. She knew, no matter what her husband had said, that he'd told more than just Joe Vigil. How else could Flavio have heard of it so soon? On top of that, she wasn't sure who was worse, Will for thinking someone had stuck a hand in a wall, or Felipe for suggesting that an adobe wall was a good place for someone to bury a child. Not for the first time, she wondered why men were allowed to do anything by themselves. She didn't bother to mention either of these things, not wanting to spend any more of the morning growing frustrated with her husband's answers.

Now she asked, "How did Manuela García come to call Will in the first place?" Like Felipe, she knew next to nothing about the woman. She knew that she lived alone somewhere near the south edge of the village, but that was about it. She never saw her anywhere and hadn't ever heard much of anything about her. In fact, she was a little surprised the old woman was still alive.

Felipe shrugged. "How should I know?" he said. "Maybe she got his name from the lumberyard. Maybe a neighbor told her. Who cares why she called him?"

"Well," Elena said, leaning back in her chair, her coffee cup cradled in her lap. "I think you did the right thing. I think Will should tell Manuela what he found and then stay away from there."

Felipe raised his arms and then let them drop. "That's what I told him," he said, although he was no longer sure exactly what he'd told Will to do. He remembered telling him to tell Manuela, but he wasn't so sure about the keeping away from there part. "I told him it was probably one of her relatives, so why should he mess with it? But you know how Will gets sometimes."

Even though Felipe and Will had worked together for so long, Elena seldom forgot that Will wasn't from the village, that before Guadalupe he'd had a whole other life that she could not even imagine. And no matter how long he'd been here, or what family he'd married into, or how much Spanish he'd picked up, she had always sensed there was something inside him that she would never know, something he never shared. Something maybe he himself didn't know was there. There had been a few times when they'd been together, when no one was watching, that Elena would see Will's eyes move away and stare off as if something was there that no one else could see. And whatever it was, it felt sad to her and old, as if it went further back than his life in Guadalupe. And she knew that Felipe had never seen it and would never understand it if she were to speak of it.

"Yes," she said to him now. "I know how Will is."

"Well," Felipe said, thinking that this conversation was over. "I think I'll go outside." He dragged his feet up, reached for his coffee and finished it off. He made as if to get up from the table. "Maybe I can get something done," he said.

"Before you go," Elena said, "maybe you can tell me what you're going to do about this."

"Me?" Felipe said. "What can I do? I just helped Will out a little. It's his problem, not mine."

"I don't mean about that," Elena said. "I mean about Flavio. What are you going to tell him?"

Felipe had almost forgotten about that old man who had called earlier, who had started this whole thing. "I'm not going to tell him anything," he said. "I'll call him and tell him to talk to Will. It's his stupid job, let him talk to Flavio."

"He doesn't want to talk to Will," Elena said. "You know that. He wants to talk to you."

For a moment, Felipe didn't say a word. Then he turned his head and looked out the open door. He could see the sun lying hot on the bare dirt that had once been grass and the lilac bush by his truck that hadn't bloomed in two years because it lived in a place where it never rained. He could see the standing posts to the portal he was going to have so much time to build, and he thought that nothing ever happens the way you think it will. Here he was with so much time on his hands and all he'd done was bits and pieces of this and that. He wondered why he'd ever let Will talk him into quitting work like it was for his own good. And now, here he was having to deal with his neighbor about something that he had nothing to do with. He looked back at Elena.

"I don't know what I'm going to say to Flavio," he said. "I don't even know why he cares about this." He pushed up to his feet. He suddenly felt tired, and thought that if Elena wasn't here he'd go back to bed. "I'll call him later," he said.

"You know he'll call back," Elena said. "Or walk up the hill looking for you."

"Yes, yes," Felipe said, waving an arm and walking out the door. "I know that."

Will was sitting back against the west wall in the middle room of the old García house. His legs were spread apart and stretched straight out on the floor. His head was resting against the sill of the window. He wasn't sure, nor did he much care what time it was, but by the hollow, empty ache in his stomach, he figured it had to be somewhere around noon.

I've been here for hours, he thought, and closed his eyes. His clothes were covered with dust, and his skin itched from the dirt and bits of straw that had leaked under his shirt. A couple of knuckles on his right hand were torn and bleeding, and every so often that hand would open and close slowly. He was smoking a cigarette, the smoke drifting out the open window behind him. He opened his eyes and looked at the gaping hole he'd made in the wall opposite him.

"This has been one rotten morning," he said out loud in the empty house.

When Will had started digging the adobe away from the four small bones, he hadn't had the slightest idea of what his morning was about to turn into. He couldn't even come up with one good reason why he was doing it, other than just falling to the place of what he wanted to see.

It had been easy digging. The adobe around the fingers was loose and dry, and Will could tell that Felipe had been right. The wall, at some time, had been opened up and the body placed in it. Then enough mud had been packed over and around it that the surface of the wall could be plastered smoothly. If it hadn't been for years of roof leaks and Will taking on the job, no one would ever have known what was there.

After an hour or so, he'd dug enough away that the hand was exposed. The four fingers curled inward, the thumb resting almost gently on top of them. He could see the small bones in the wrist and how the rest of the body was farther back in the wall. He brought his own hand close. His fingers were almost twice the length of those he'd uncovered. They didn't look white now but were stained gray as if, over time, dirt and moisture had leached into them.

Will lowered his arm and rested his hand on his thigh. He knelt there, staring at them for a moment and then reached just above them and pulled loose a chunk of adobe the size of his fist. Behind it was another one, and when he pulled it loose, a stream of dirt and small chunks of adobe fell in a rush to the floor. He turned his head away from the cloud of dust, and when he looked back he could see a trail of cloth hanging in the opening.

What is that? he thought, leaning closer. A black widow the size of his thumbnail crawled along one edge of it and disappeared in a seam in the adobe behind it. Grimacing, Will reached out and pulled on it. The fabric ripped, and inside it Will could make out the small thin bones of five toes. He fell backwards and, using his hands, slid back to the far wall.

Now, he took a long, slow hit off his cigarette and dropped his hand to the dirt floor. The draft coming in the lower part of the window was warm on the back of his head. His knuckles were throbbing, and he wondered vaguely when he had scraped them. The hand he had uncovered earlier was hidden beneath the dirt that had fallen. But what he could see was a two-foot by two-foot hole in the wall across from him. And near the top of it was the skeleton of yet another child, hanging there motionless in that dark space.

I'm in a graveyard, Will thought, the cigarette burning forgotten now between his fingers. A place where someone buried children. He moved his eyes slowly over the wall across from him, and somehow he knew that there were more than just two children buried in the walls of this house.

# ELEVEN

✠ **IT WAS EARLY AFTERNOON,** and Manuela García was at her kitchen window watching Will walk down the hill from her grandfather's house. His toolbag was slung over one shoulder. He held a shovel in one hand and walked through the sagebrush with it as if it were a cane. She thought that he looked like an old man who was tired of his life.

"You know, don't you?" she said out loud. The santo of the boy stood on the windowsill and he, too, watched Will make his way down the hill. And even from so far away, the two of them could see that Will's face was streaked with dirt and that his clothes were filthy.

Manuela had heard him come to the door that morning, heard him pound on the door, heard his hand rattle the doorknob. She had slept poorly through the night, her sleep plagued by bad dreams with dark, shadowy things in them, and when she heard Will, she was confused for a moment, thinking that somehow it was her grandfather.

He had come to the house in much the same way. The only real difference, she thought, was that it was never early in the day that he came, but always near dark. She would hear the door to the house open, his boots passing down the hallway, and then the deep, muffled sound of his voice as he talked to her father. After that, it would be quiet for a long, long moment, as if everything in the house was waiting. It was so quiet that Manuela could hear the creak of each single floorboard, and the hiss of the kerosene lamp, and the skittering of a rodent in the ceiling above her bed. And then the doorknob would twist and turn, and the door to her room would swing open.

How old was I? Manuela wondered. Nine? Twelve? Thirty? Then she realized that, of course, she had been all those ages. And just before leaving her, her grandfather would stand by the bed and, slowly buttoning his trousers, would look down at her as a child and a young girl and a woman.

"Do you want me to leave, hija?" he would say, his breath still ragged and coming too fast. He would reach out and cup the side of her face, his hand calloused and thick, the cracks in the skin grimed with dirt.

"No," Manuela would say, knowing this is what he wanted to hear. "I want you to stay," and she would say this when she was nine years old and twelve and thirty. Always the same words. And sometimes they were true, and sometimes, especially when he'd forgotten to bring her a gift, or when he'd hurt her, bruised her with the weight of his body, or his movements were so frantic that he had struck her, they were a lie. What she wanted was for him to go away.

She remembered asking him once why her mother had left her. Where she had gone that night with Rosalie. The old man had stared at her silently for a long time, so long that Manuela had wished the question she had asked could be taken back. Finally, his voice low and harsh, he said, "I don't know where she went. All I know is she left us. She took your sister and ran away into the night." Then he went to the doorway, and before leaving, he looked back at her. "Your mother has forgotten about us," he said, "and your sister does not even remember your name. Never ask me about this again. Do you understand, hija?"

"Yes, grandfather," Manuela had said to him.

When she heard Will at the door that morning, she'd almost called out to him. Almost said, "Come in, hijo. I'm here in bed waiting for you." But then she heard him move away from the house. And moments later, when there was no sound of his truck engine, she knew that he had gone up the hill to her grandfather's house.

Will was near the bottom of the hill now. He was walking slowly, staring down at the ground, swinging the shovel forward with each step he took. Once he was clear of the sage, he paused for a moment and shifted the toolbag, as if it had been digging into his skin. When he began walking again, Manuela turned from the window. She filled the coffee pot with water, placed it on the stove, and then hurried through the house to the front door.

As soon as she opened it, she could see that he was near his truck. She watched him swing his toolbag off his shoulder and toss it, along with the shovel, into the bed of the pickup. He bent over and brushed some of the dust and dirt off his pants. Then he straightened up slowly, as if the muscles in his back were tight and strained, and pulled his shirt loose and shook it until whatever bits of dirt and straw that were inside fell loose. Then he turned his head and looked over at the house.

"Yes, hijo, I'm here," the old woman whispered, smiling. "Venga aquí. I have some coffee on the stove for you." And when he took a step toward the house, she backed away from the door. And a second later, sure that he was coming, she went back to the kitchen to wait for him.

"Sit down, hijo," the old woman said. "I made coffee for us."

Will was standing in the doorway to the kitchen. The lights were on in the room, and the curtains over the window were pulled back. On the windowsill, in full sun, was what looked like a santo. It was facing the window and was too far away for Will to tell if it was the carved figure of Christ, or the Virgin Mary, or some other saint. He hadn't seen it in the house before and wondered where it had come from. His old neighbor, Telesfor Ruiz, had told him stories about them. About how they'd been kept in homes until the church had outlawed them. And then, the old man told Will, they'd been given to the priest who had burned them. Burned them all beneath the cottonwood that grew beside the church.

"You have a santo," Will said.

The old woman was at the stove with her back to him. She glanced over her shoulder and saw where he was looking. "No," she said. "He's not a santo. There are no santos in this house. My grandfather carved him and gave him to me when I was a girl." Then she smiled and turned back to the stove.

She was wearing the same nightgown she'd worn before with a thin sweater thrown over it. The fabric was so worn that her elbows, thin and chaffed, stuck out through the cloth. The cuffs were frayed and dirty, and when she'd turned Will could see that the top buttons were missing. Her hair was unbrushed and hung loose. Her feet and legs were bare, and the sight of them made him feel uncomfortable, as if yet again he was seeing more of her than he should, as if she had purposely chosen this for him to see.

Who are you? he wondered. Are you the woman who managed to get everything she wanted from me the first day we met? Or the one who was so cold and distant to Felipe? Or are you this one, the one who makes me coffee and offers me food and who looks at me sometimes as if there is no line between us and anything could happen in this house?

He watched as she went to the refrigerator and took out a carton of milk. Then, still stooped down, she looked up at him.

"Sit down, hijo," she said again.

Will shook his head slightly. "I wasn't going to stay long."

"If you weren't going to stay," she said, and the words rushed from her mouth, "then you should not have bothered to come." And just like that Will could feel something shift in the air between them.

There, he thought. I know this woman. Lowering his head, he stepped into the room, went to the table, and pulled out a chair. "All right," he said, sitting down. "I'll have a cup of coffee with you."

"Thank you, hijo," the old woman said, and straightened up slowly. She brought two cups to the table and then put the carton of milk off to the side. She sat down across from him and folded her arms. The skin above her breasts was marked with age and meshed with fine lines.

"So," she said, "you went to my grandfather's house."

For a moment, Will just sat there looking at her. The room suddenly felt too warm, and he could feel the quiet in the house pushing in on him. He picked up the coffee cup and took a sip. Like before, it tasted stale and burnt. He put it down carefully.

"Yes," he said, finally. "I went up to your grandfather's house." Then he moved his eyes away and looked out the window at the old house up on the hill. Just the sight of it sitting up there made him want to get up and leave. He didn't want to tell this old woman about what he'd found and what it might mean. All he really wanted to do was go home to Estrella and his girls and forget this day had even happened. He looked back across the table at Manuela García and let out a soft breath.

"There's something wrong up there," he said.

The old woman opened her mouth to speak and then closed it. Will saw her arms tighten around her chest and her fingers press deeper into her skin. Then she dropped her arms. She folded her hands together and smiled.

Will had been in Tito's Bar one afternoon with Felipe and Eli Ortega when two guys suddenly began fighting. It didn't last long. One of them hit the other, and when the man who'd been struck got up off the floor his face was bloodied, and he had that same smile that was on Manuela García's face. A little dazed, a little lost, a little like not much at all had happened. Just looking at the guy had made Will feel bad.

And though he didn't feel quite the same way now, still the look on Manuela García's face made him think that either what he'd said was too big for her to grasp or that she hadn't heard a word he'd said. He leaned forward and put his arms on the table.

"I found something up there," he said to her. "I found the bones of two children buried in the wall of your grandfather's house."

After a few seconds, still smiling, she said, "There are always things to find in old houses."

And when she said it, a chill crept up Will's spine and he leaned back a little. From somewhere in the house, he heard a faint rustling noise. Like it came from outside or from behind one of the closed doors, a rustle of leaves or a flutter of papers. It lasted for only a little while, and then it was gone.

"Not things like this," he said.

Manuela unfolded her hands and dropped them to her lap. She turned her head a little and arched her neck so that the skin there tightened. For a second Will could glimpse the young woman she once was, and he knew she had done this purposely. What he didn't know was why. He remembered thinking that first time they'd met that he'd missed something. He realized now that he'd missed everything.

"Manuela," he said, and it was the first time he'd spoken her name. "You knew, didn't you? You knew all along what was up there."

"Did I know?" she asked softly. "I don't know what I knew, hijo." She lowered her head slowly and looked at him, and now she looked old and tired and used. "I have a story to tell you," she said. "Unless you wish to leave." And here she paused before asking, "Do you want to hear it?"

The house was still now. The carving of the boy stood on the windowsill. Will had the sense that the boy was waiting to see what he would say.

"Yes," he said, finally. "Tell me."

"In all these years, I have only been to my grandfather's house twice," the old woman said. "The last time was just after his death. I was a woman then and it was cold and raining. The first time I went there I was a little girl, just nine years old. And I'll tell you what happened that day, mi hijo."

It was a warm day in early August when Manuela walked through the sagebrush to her grandfather's house. Her father had left the village early the day before to shear sheep for the Quintana family up north. He told his daughter that since they had so many sheep and that none had been sheared in the spring, he was not sure when he would return.

Manuela had gotten up early and spent most of the morning doing her chores. She made her bed and straightened her room. She washed all the dishes, cleaned the counters, and swept and mopped all the floors. Her father cared little for what was around him, but when her grandfather came to see her, his mood would darken if things were out of place—if her clothes were on the floor, or her bed unmade, or if there was dust behind the open doors. And if that happened, he would keep the gift he had brought for her, or rip the buttons from her dress when he unclothed her. And after he was gone, she would have to sew together what he had torn.

When the house was clean, she went to the kitchen. She sat down at the table, and ate a stale tortilla with honey that she had made two days before. Her legs were crossed at the ankle, and she swung them back and forth a little bit. As she sat there eating, she glimpsed movement outside the window and saw that her grandfather had just stepped from the door of his house.

At first, she thought that he was coming to visit her and that she should eat quickly and hurry to her room and wait for him. But then she saw him walk away from the house. She got up from the table and went to the window. She pressed against the edge of the sink and stood up on her toes. She watched him make his way through the sagebrush and disappear into the piñon trees south of the clearing.

She stood like that for a long time, the muscles in her legs straining, her eyes moving now and then from the empty clearing to the house and back again to the line of trees. Behind her, other than the faint rustling sound of the rodents in the ceiling above her room, the house was quiet. And although the day outside was still in full sun, she could sense that already the shadows were growing darker inside the house.

After a while longer, Manuela dropped to the soles of her feet. Then she walked through the house, stepped out the front door, and went to the base of the hill.

"Why?" Will asked.

The old woman started slightly, startled that Will had asked anything. "Why?" she asked.

"Yes," he said. He thought that there were a couple of other

160

questions he could have asked. Like, where was her mother? Not to mention that part about an old man undressing his granddaughter. But he had a feeling that if he asked those, this story would either end or go somewhere else. Later, he thought, I can ask those things later. "Yes," he said, again. "Why did you go up there?"

"To see," she said. "You of all people should understand that. Now let me go on, hijo, with my story."

She followed the path that wound up the hill through the sagebrush. Every so often, Manuela could see the mark of her grandfather's boots in the soft dirt. Above her, the sky was blue and clear. The clearing behind the house was quiet and still. She could smell the sharp, bitter scent of sage as she brushed against it.

When she came to the top of the slope, she stopped near the edge of the pit just outside the west wall of the house. Inside it, she could see empty, rusted cans and broken bottles and rough-cut shards of metal and the carcass of a large, white dog. Dirt had been thrown over the animal, but she could still see one of its hind legs and part of its skull. She could hear the raspy hum of flies and yellow jackets. She wondered what the dog had done for her grandfather to have shot it. She wondered why he had dragged it all the way back to his house.

The windows facing her were all closed, and a curtain hung over each one. She trailed her hand on the wall as she walked along the side of the house. The door by which her grandfather had left the house was closed and latched. The wood was thick and weathered black in places. As she stood before it, she heard, from not far away, the song of a single bird. Its call was sharp and clear, and as quickly as it had come, it was gone. She reached out, slid the latch up, and pushed against the door with the flat of her hand. As it swung open slowly, she could smell mud and old smoke and the strong, bitter scent of her grandfather.

"The first thing I saw, hijo, was the room at the far end of the house. My eyes didn't see so good from the sun, so I didn't see those crosses you found hanging on the wall." Through all of this telling, Manuela's eyes would sometimes move around the room, as if somehow she could remember better that way. But now she was looking at Will and smiling a little. She leaned across the table and touched his hand.

"Would you like more coffee?" she asked.

"No," Will said. His cup was still half full. He'd forgotten all about it. He picked it up and sipped at it. "Were you afraid?" he asked.

Manuela pulled her hand back. "Of my grandfather's house?" she said. "No," and this she said slower, "I wasn't afraid. I was something, hijo, but it wasn't that."

What she could make out in the far room was a large table in the center and a stack of shadowed shelves against the wall behind it. She could see that a chair was tipped over in front of the table, as if her grandfather had left in a hurry and hadn't bothered to stand it back up. All she could see of the middle room was a stretch of the clean swept dirt floor.

Manuela took a step forward and stopped in the shade of the doorway. A heatstove stood in the corner to the left. A cast-iron pot, the wood handle charred, rested on top of it, and a black stovepipe ran up from it and through the ceiling. The walls were mud plastered and bare, and here, too, the dirt floor was swept clean. The bed where Manuela thought her grandfather must sleep was pushed up against the wall off to her right. It was narrow and quilted, and laid out on it was a pair of pants and a shirt torn at the shoulder and one shoe, and, scattered about, a handful of coins, a small pocket knife, two flat stones, and a cube of sugar coated with dirt.

As Manuela stood staring at what lay on the bed she could see that the clothes were far too small to fit her grandfather. They might fit her, but she had never once worn pants, and her grandfather would never wish to see her in a shirt that was so badly torn. And besides, of what use would just one shoe be?

"Where did your clothes come from?" she wondered aloud. "And why are you in my grandfather's house?" She looked again at the far end of the house, at the chair lying on its side. The house was dead still. A little sunlight crept in around the edges of the curtains. She thought of walking through the house and standing the chair back on its legs, but the thought of passing through the middle room made her uneasy. She glanced back at the bed. And then she stepped into the room and sat down on the very edge of the quilt.

The trousers were beside her, and she ran her fingers over the loops around the waist and then down each leg. They were crusted, as if something had spilled and dried on them, and badly worn at the knees. The bottoms were cuffed, and she ran her fingers inside each one, feeling bits of dirt and sand stuck there.

Some boy wore these, she thought. Some boy who couldn't even keep them clean. She dug her hands in the pockets and felt around. They were empty. She picked up the shirt and held it in front of her. It was ripped from the neck down to one shoulder. She thought that if she had her needle and thread she could mend it so that he could wear it again. She ran her hand over the one shoe and felt how thin the sole was, the laces missing some of the eyelets, the ends of them frayed. She touched each coin, opened and closed the knife, felt how smooth the stones were, and touched her tongue to the cube of sugar. Then she put everything back as it had been. She folded her hands in her lap and sat there looking at what she had found.

"And that's when I heard a noise, hijo," the old woman said. She had been going on in a straightforward manner, and it took Will a moment to realize she was talking to him.

"What kind of noise?" he asked.

"Oh, just a noise. It startled me a little because the house had been so still." She moved her eyes away and looked past him, almost as if someone was standing in the doorway to the kitchen. "I had a sister once," she said. "Did you know that?"

"No," Will said. "I didn't know that."

"Her name was Rosalie, and my mother took her away one night. She took her out into a bad snowstorm and they never came back. My grandfather told me that they ran away and left me." She looked at Will now and smiled. "Sometimes, I can see them. I see them living in a small house with a garden beside a big river. A big river of water. When I think of them, hijo, I see them there. And Rosalie always asks the same question. She asks, 'Is it true, mama, I once had a sister?'"

Will half closed his eyes and let out a long, soft breath. "What happened in that house, Manuela?" he asked.

"What house, hijo?"

"Your grandfather's house."

"Oh, yes," she said, nodding her head. "My grandfather's house. Did I tell you there was a noise?"

"Yes, you told me that. Was it your grandfather?"

The old woman grunted softly. "No, hijo," she said, moving a little in her chair. "It wasn't my grandfather. It was a boy."

He was a scrawny, little boy, not even as big as she was, with skinny arms and legs, his chest so thin she could see each of his ribs. His skin was dark, his hair lightened a little from the sun. He was wearing only a pair of underwear that were grass stained. His face was streaked with dirt, and Manuela thought he looked as if he'd been crying.

"What are you doing in my grandfather's house?" she said.

"I'm looking for my brother," the boy said, not even looking at her. "And I can't find him." His voice was a little harsh, a little rough, like he'd been crying for a long time.

"This is my grandfather's house," Manuela said again. "You shouldn't be here. And I don't even know you. How would I know your brother?"

"There were so many fish in the creek," the boy said. "I remember that," and then he shivered as if he was freezing cold. "I don't want to be here," he said, and he began to cry.

"Then you should leave," Manuela said, and she stood up.

"I miss my brother," he said. His face was wet, and mucus ran from his nose.

Manuela looked out the open door. She could see the swing hanging from the piñon tree. Beyond that was the empty, quiet stretch of sagebrush. She thought her grandfather might be coming back soon and that she should leave. She looked back at the boy. He was just standing there. He was standing there still crying.

I never cry, she thought to herself. And then she said, "I have to go now."

And that was when the boy looked at her. His eyes were wet and dark. He had a thin face, and it made her suddenly think of the carved boy in her bed. "Can I go with you?" he asked her.

For a second, she had wondered. But then she said, "No, I already have a boy. But you should go before my grandfather finds you here." And then she turned, stepped outside into the sunlight, and walked back down the hill to her house.

"There, mi hijo," Manuela García said to Will. "That's the story I wanted to tell you."

165

Will sat in his chair looking at her. Her voice had grown stronger the longer she talked, and now she was sitting across from him with a small smile on her face, her posture straight, her hands folded on top of the table. He knew there was more to the story she'd told him. He didn't know what it was, but it was far more than some chance meeting between two children in some old adobe. There was something else nagging at him about the boy she'd described, but he let that go for now.

"Who was he?" he asked.

The old woman shrugged slightly. "How should I know?" she said. "Some boy. Some boy that no one wanted." And the way she phrased that made Will wonder just what she meant.

"I don't understand," he said. "I don't understand what you mean."

The old woman looked down at the table, at the coffee cup he'd forgotten about. "Would you like more coffee, hijo?"

"No," Will said. "I'm fine."

"Are you hungry?"

"No," he said. "I don't want to eat anything."

She raised her eyes and looked at him. "If you want to understand, then you need to ask the right question. Do you even know what that is?"

"No," he said, shaking his head. "I don't." He could feel himself getting angry, and he pushed against it knowing it wouldn't do him any good in this house.

"Then let me help you," Manuela said, leaning over the table. "Ask me what happened the second time I went to my grandfather's house and maybe then you'll understand."

Possibly for the first time in Will's life it occurred to him that there might be some things that were best left alone. He could almost hear Felipe whisper in his ear, "Just get up and leave now, jodido. What are you waiting for? Leave this crazy old woman and we'll go drink some beer."

166

Smiling a little, Will reached for a cigarette and then dropped his hand. "All right," he said. "What happened? What happened the second time you went up to that old house?"

It was twenty years later when Manuela García walked back up the hill to her grandfather's house, and this had happened just one week after Bolivar García had been found dead in the woods. Ray Pacheco, the Guadalupe police officer, had told her about his death and had gone on to say that instead of bringing the body to the Guadalupe cemetery, they'd buried him where they found him, in a sparse growth of piñon trees near the creek. He'd given her the old man's coat and the little money he'd had in his pockets. Then, without saying much more, he'd driven off in the village truck.

Two days later, Manuela put on a black dress and, carrying her grandfather's coat in a burlap bag, went up the hill to the old house. It was cold and raining, and clouds hung low over the mountains. The walls of the house were stained dark from moisture. The eaves ran with water, and the path through the sagebrush was slick and muddy.

This time, Manuela didn't pause by the pit in front of the house but walked directly to the south door. Once again, though, she stood before it for a moment. Her hair and dress were soaked with rain, and her legs and the hem of her dress were splattered with mud. She could smell the strong odor of wet burlap.

Finally, she reached out, pulled up the latch, and pushed the door open.

"I was just going to throw his coat inside, hijo," she said to Will. "That's all I wanted to do. I didn't want it in my house smelling of him."

When the door was fully open, Manuela took a step closer and, with both her hands, threw the coat onto the dirt floor. Whether it was because of the gray day or that the curtains were open, Manuela could see clearly to the far end of the house. She could see that the chair that had been tipped over twenty years before was pushed up close to the table. She could see that on top of the table was a large pile of what looked like sticks and pieces of wood. She leaned forward and peered into the shadows.

And that was when, from some hidden place in the middle room of the house, the boy suddenly appeared. He was wearing the same filthy underwear and was still so thin Manuela could see each of his ribs. His face was dirty and dry, as if he'd stopped his crying a long time ago. Manuela stood just outside the doorway, the top half of her body leaning in, her hands reaching out as if frozen in place. And then she heard him speak in the same voice she had heard before.

"Can I come with you?" he asked. "Take me with you so I can find my brother."

# TWELVE

AT A LITTLE BEFORE NOON that same day, Felipe found himself sitting in the cab of his truck in front of Flavio Montoya's house. Instead of walking the quarter mile down the hill to his neighbor's place, he'd driven one big circle, almost halfway around the village, to end up pretty much where he'd started.

Just like my whole stupid life, Felipe thought.

Up the hill, he could see his own house. He could see where his sad, little garden was. He could see the faded metal on his roof and the cracked, gray plastered walls that should have been color coated way back in June. And here he was sitting in his neighbor's driveway like he didn't have anything better to do.

After walking out of his house, he'd gone to his garden and dug up the remaining potatoes, which weren't enough to fill his front pockets. Every so often, Elena had come out of the house, once to hang the laundry on the line by the pile of firewood, another time to shake the dust out of the small rug in the bathroom. And each time, she didn't say one word to her husband, knowing that if there was one thing Felipe would listen to, it was silence. Finally, after she'd gone back inside the house the second time, she'd heard his truck door slam and the grind of the engine turning over. Then she'd gone to the window in her living room that looked out over the valley and waited, her arms crossed, until she saw his truck pull into Flavio Montoya's driveway. Then, shaking her head, she'd gone to the kitchen to check on the chili that was cooking on the stove.

Felipe looked over at Flavio's house. It was a well-kept adobe with a shingled roof. Off in the back was a small grove of apple trees, the leaves yellowed and red and just beginning to fall. The car Flavio's wife, Martha, used to drive before she died was parked in the shade by an old shed. Both front tires had gone flat, and the windshield was covered with dirt and bird droppings.

Felipe wondered what the old man wanted. Although they'd been pretty good neighbors forever, it wasn't like they'd ever been close friends. Besides that, he didn't like unexpected things popping up in his life without his knowing it. It made him uneasy and gave him the sense that nothing could be trusted. He pictured himself as a quiet, simple man whose pleasures came from getting up early every morning and eating his breakfast in peace and then driving to work where he'd spend the next eight to ten hours with a bunch of guys until it was finally time to drink a few beers. And after that, he'd go home to his family and eat the beans and chili Elena had made. And then, tired from working so hard, he'd go to bed and start the whole thing over the next morning.

That's all I want, he often thought to himself. I just want a life where nothing happens. But in truth, with three grown sons who lived not far away and eight grandchildren and a wife like Elena who seemed to notice every little thing he did, his life was more often than not one long series of unexpected events.

And then there was Will, he thought, and he blew out a sigh. Will was a whole other thing. He remembered the time Will had started up one big mess about some story he'd heard about a gringa that had been found hanging naked from a bridge in the middle of nowhere. Felipe didn't even like remembering that time. The entire village had not only tried to kill Will, but had blamed Felipe for telling Will the stupid story in the first place. And now here he was again, in the middle of another of Will's problems.

"I don't know about you sometimes, jodido," Felipe muttered to himself. Then he hit the truck horn lightly and got out of his pickup to go see what his neighbor wanted.

The first thing that went through Flavio Montoya's mind when he heard Felipe hit the horn and saw the truck door swing open was, Eee, finally.

When Flavio had seen his neighbor drive up to his house, he'd hurried into his kitchen and put on a pot of coffee. Then he'd gone back into the living room only to see that his neighbor was still sitting in the cab of his pickup and having a conversation with someone who wasn't there.

What was even worse was that the longer Flavio stared out the window, the more he regretted calling Felipe in the first place. What had seemed like a good idea when he'd gotten out of bed that morning now seemed foolish. A quiet rush of fatigue went through him, and he thought he was like some old man who couldn't even keep his few memories to himself. As he watched Felipe walk toward the house, he thought that he would have a cup of coffee with his neighbor and tell him he was sorry to have bothered him.

Felipe hadn't seen much of Flavio Montoya since the old man's wife had died a little over a year ago. Every so often, he'd caught sight of him out with his cows or over at his sister's abandoned house irrigating her alfalfa field, but he couldn't even remember the last time they'd talked. And seeing him now made Felipe feel bad that he had left his neighbor alone for so long.

Flavio looked like he'd had a tough go of it. His face was grayer, and the lines in his skin looked deeper. His eyes were bloodshot, the skin beneath them dark and swollen. On top of that, he seemed smaller and there was a tired feel about him that Felipe didn't remember him having.

"Cómo está, Flavio?" Felipe said, smiling and taking the old man's hand lightly. "I haven't seen you in a long time."

"I'm fine, Felipe," Flavio said. "I'm fine." He shook his head and looked down. "I want to apologize, though, for bothering you. I didn't want you to go to all this trouble."

"Don't even say that," Felipe said. "It's no trouble to visit a neighbor. When Elena told me you called, I figured it was a good reason to come see you."

"You sure you got the time?" Flavio asked. He was feeling a little better, not quite so foolish. He thought it might be okay to have a cup of coffee with a neighbor he'd always liked, even if he seldom saw him.

Felipe hissed and raised both arms. "That's all I have," he said.

The kitchen was a bright, well-lit room. A large window looked out over the grove of twisted apple trees. The counters were clean, everything put away. The floor was white linoleum. It felt to Felipe, like a room the old man didn't use much anymore. He pulled out a chair and sat at the table while Flavio brought over two cups.

"How's your family doing?" the old man asked. "I see those grandchildren of yours running all over." He sat down, reached forward, and slid a cup over to Felipe.

"They're all fine," Felipe said. "They keep getting bigger, but they're all good." He almost asked about Flavio's own family, but managed to catch himself in time. With his sister and Martha both dead now, and the fact that they'd been childless, there wasn't much of a family left for Flavio to talk about. Felipe picked up the cup of coffee and took a sip. It was so weak he could see the bottom of the cup. "The coffee's good," he said.

"Bueno," the old man said. "Do you need some milk?"

"No, this is fine."

"So how have you been?"

"Not so bad," Felipe said. "I took some time off of work to get things done around the house. If I'm lucky I'll get it plastered before winter." He knew he should ask the old man how things had been since his wife died, but he'd never been much good at those kinds of things. He wished he'd brought Elena along. She had a way of asking the right questions and wasn't afraid of the answers. He could have drunk his coffee in peace while the two of them talked about Martha and whatever else it was the old man had on his mind.

"Did you hear about Delfino?" Flavio asked, leaning back in his chair.

"No," Felipe said, and the first thought he had was that yet another viejo from the village had died. "What happened to him?"

"Oh, he had some trouble with his neighbor," Flavio said, slowly stretching out a leg, like all the bones in his knee ached. "I guess his pigs got out again and killed Juju Padilla's dog."

For a second, Felipe thought this could be the beginning of a conversation he might be having with Will. He thought that he'd have to tell Will about this, if he ever saw that jodido again. He took another sip of coffee. "How do pigs kill a dog?" he asked. "I thought it was the other way around."

Flavio shrugged. "I don't know how they did it," he said. "Delfino didn't see it happen. All he saw was them eating it after."

"I would get rid of those pigs if I was him," Felipe said. "Besides, how does a pig outrun a dog?"

"It was a little dog. One of those that bark at nothing. I guess Juju's not too happy about it." He turned his head and looked out the window. "Maybe it's the weather making everything a little crazy. I've never seen it like this. Never. My cows are always thirsty, and all my sister's alfalfa field grew were weeds."

"Eee, don't tell me," Felipe said, still a little stuck on how a pig could catch a dog, even a little dog. "It was the same with my garden. The chilis didn't even bloom. And those potatoes."

"Potatoes need those long rains so the water can sink into the ground," Flavio said. "We don't get those anymore. I remember when it would start raining on the Fourth of July, and it wouldn't quit until the middle of August. You could count on it every year, and then we'd get the first snow in October." He shook his head. "I don't know sometimes. I don't know how things can change so much. Sometimes, I wonder if what I remember is even true."

"Well," Felipe said, not quite sure what to say to that. "I don't know about the weather, either. But it's pretty damn dry, all right." He was beginning to feel as if maybe Elena had, once again, made a big deal out of nothing, that all Flavio wanted was a little company so he could talk about Delfino's pigs and reminisce about the weather. He thought that he'd finish his coffee and start thinking about how to say goodbye without looking like he wanted to leave.

The old man was still looking out the window. Between the branches of the apple trees, Felipe could glimpse his own house sitting up on the hill. He wondered what Elena was doing, if she even knew he was here. He picked up his coffee cup. "I needed this coffee," he said, just to say something.

"I don't make it too strong anymore," Flavio said, absently. "I'm glad it tastes good." Then he drew his leg back up and shifted in his chair. "There's something I wanted to ask you, Felipe," he said. "I was going to forget about it, but I don't want to think about it later. I wanted to ask you about that little boy you found."

Though the expression on Felipe's face didn't change, what he was thinking did. His first thought was the same one he'd had earlier, which was how in hell did he end up in Flavio Montoya's kitchen when this was all Will's fault. The second was where did Flavio get the idea that it was a little boy buried in the wall of that old house that he never wanted to hear about again. And the last was that he was going to have one big talk with that fucking jodido Eli Ortega when he got out of here. And with all those things going through his mind, about all Felipe could think of to say was, "Qué little boy?"

"The little boy I heard you found," Flavio said. He reached up and rubbed at the side of his face and then put his hand back in his lap. "Manuel Cisneros told me about it."

"Manuel Cisneros told you?" Felipe said. Manuel Cisneros was married to Eli's wife's sister. Not for the first time, Felipe wondered why people weren't smart enough to keep their mouths shut about everything.

"Yes, Manuel. You know him. He works at the mine. He's married to one of those Sanchez girls."

"Oh sí," Felipe said, shaking his head hard. "What was I thinking? Of course I know Manuel." He had no idea where this was going, but every part of his being told him to make it go away, to make it less than it was, whatever the hell that was. He shrugged his shoulders. "I don't know how Manuel heard about this, but he got everything wrong. First, I didn't find nothing. It was that guy I used to work with found it. I just helped him out a little. He thought he'd found some old bones on a jobsite he's working. I told him it didn't look like much to me. You know how those willow branches can look sometimes. I told him to plaster over them and forget about it." He made a face. "I don't know how stories get so crazy around here. But you know how people are."

Felipe leaned back in his chair thinking, there, that's done with. He thought that when he got home, he would tell Elena that he had seen Flavio and then maybe get some work in on that portal. He picked up his coffee and finished it off. "Why did you want to know, anyway?" he asked. And as soon as the words came out of his mouth, he could hear his wife's voice.

"You never learn, do you, Felipe?" her voice said. "I don't know how you always manage to say the wrong thing at the wrong time. When I'm mad, you want to joke around. When I'm happy, you say something stupid to make me angry. When Flavio is about to say goodbye, you ask him a question like that. Do you ever think about what might happen?"

Flavio slid his coffee cup off to one side. He put his hands on the table and folded them together. His fingers were thick, the nails broken, old scabs marked his skin.

"I'm glad you asked me that, Felipe," he said. "Because a long time ago I had a nephew. He was just a boy. Little Jose was his name, and one day he disappeared. And for years I wondered how my nephew could disappear in a village as small as this one. I always felt that somehow he was still here. Somewhere just beyond my reach."

176

# THIRTEEN

✽BY NOON, ESTRELLA HAD STOPPED wondering where Will was and was beginning to worry about where he was. Hadn't he said he was just going to talk to that Manuela García woman and would be back soon? How could anything so simple be taking so long? She knew that a hundred things could have happened. Will could have run into Felipe on his way home, or gotten involved with Joe Vigil and all those other men who spent hours drinking coffee and talking about nothing at the lumberyard. For all she knew, one of his bald rear tires that he was too stubborn to replace could have finally gone flat. She told herself that anything might have happened and that there was no real reason for her to worry. But still, she wished he was home with her. Not only so she could stop worrying, but also because she'd had one bad morning and needed to talk to him about it.

After walking the girls down the road to their bus stop, Estrella had come home and spent ten minutes putting things away in the kitchen. Then, with one more look around to see if she'd missed anything, she'd gotten in her truck and driven across the village to talk to Nana about Manuela García.

The first thing she saw when she pulled into her grandmother's drive was Monica's small car parked in the shade of a cottonwood tree. "What's she doing here?" Estrella wondered. It wasn't Monica's day to check on Nana. Besides that, she worked at the village office and had to be there by eight o'clock every morning. She never came to look in on their grandmother until her lunch break. Estrella parked beside her sister's car and shut off the engine. She pushed the truck door open and, thinking something must have happened and praying it was nothing too bad, she hurried to the house.

Monica was sitting at the kitchen table, drinking a cup of coffee and smoking a cigarette. She glanced up when Estrella came in the open door and then lowered her eyes and rubbed the butt end of her cigarette around the rim of the saucer she was using as an ashtray.

"What are you doing here?" Estrella said. "Is everything okay?"

"Everything's fine," Monica said, her voice low. "At least sort of fine. I just came over to smoke a couple of cigarettes before work."

Estrella looked around the kitchen. The door to her grandmother's room was closed. "Where's Nana?" she asked. The old woman was usually up by now moving things from one place to another.

"In bed," her sister said. "She says she's not going to get up today. She's in there lying on top of the blankets with her head up on a pillow. Every time I go in to see her, she asks who I am and then tells me one horrible story after another."

Estrella walked over to the table and sat down across from her sister. She could see threads of gray in Monica's hair, and the faint lines above her upper lip seemed deeper. Monica looked tired, and for one quick second, Estrella caught a glimpse of her as an old woman sitting alone in her own kitchen.

She buried the thought in her mind. "Something's wrong," she said. "What is it?"

Monica shook her head and, still not looking at her sister and still playing with her cigarette, said, "Did you know Nana's cousins raped her when she was a girl? And when her father found out, he beat her? He didn't beat those two monsters; he beat her." She looked up at her sister. Estrella could tell now that at some point before she'd arrived, Monica had been crying. "Did you know that?"

"Yes," Estrella said. "She told me yesterday. She told me it was another story for our book."

"Our book," Monica said softly. "Our book about our family."

"I told Will what Nana said," Estrella said, hoping this might make her sister feel better. "He told me not to worry about it. That if you look hard enough, you'd find all sorts of things in everybody's family."

"Will would say that," Monica said. She'd always liked Will. Even if she enjoyed teasing Estrella about him, she often wondered what it would be like to live with him instead of her husband. It would be different. "That's not what Lawrence said."

"You told him? I thought you were going to keep Nana's stories to yourself."

"I thought so, too," Monica said. "I had a weak moment."

"I don't like Jews," Lawrence had said. "You can't trust any of them."

He and Monica were sitting on the wood deck outside their house. It was almost seven o'clock and just beginning to get dark. From inside, Monica could hear the television, and the sounds of her three children arguing over what to watch. She'd drunk two beers and one wine cooler while listening to her husband tell her about his day mowing ditches along the side of the road for the county.

"I didn't find one thing in all those ditches worth keeping," he'd told her. "All I found was a little girl's naked doll with the hair pulled out and a ripped bra hanging in a bunch of weeds." And that was when Monica had pulled yet another beer out of the cooler beside her and told him what her grandmother had told her.

"How can you not like Jews?" Monica had said. "You don't even know any. Besides that, if what Nana said is true, you've been sleeping with one for eighteen years."

"What did he say to that?" Estrella asked.

"You know that deer in the headlights look Lawrence sometimes gets?" Monica asked.

"Yes," Estrella said, and though she tried to keep a straight face, she found herself smiling.

"It's not funny, Estrella."

"I know it's not, Monica." Her hand was in her lap, and she pinched her thigh hard to keep from laughing. "What happened then?"

Monica shook her head. "He went to Tito's, drank some whiskey, pushed Felix Sanchez off his stool for being mean to Nemecio Archuleta, and came home all drunk. He said he felt a little better because he realized that even if I was a Jew, at least our children weren't, and if they were it was so little that no one would ever notice."

Estrella wasn't sure what to say to that. She wasn't even sure if the end of the story was good or bad. "Well," she said.

"You don't have to say anything, Estrella," Monica said. "He's my husband, not yours." She stood up, picked up the saucer, went to the open doorway and threw the cigarette butts outside. Then she went to the sink and rinsed the plate. "I should get to work," she said. "I'm late as it is." She turned around, leaned back against the counter, and folded her arms across her chest. "Are you going to stay for a while?"

"Yes," Estrella said. "For a little while." She thought it might be best not to mention she planned on asking Nana about Manuela García. Her sister had enough on her mind without worrying about one more thing. "Maybe I'll try to get her out of bed," she said.

"Good luck with that," Monica said. "I don't think our grandmother is doing so good."

Estrella wanted to ask why Monica thought that, but then the sight of Nana beneath the cottonwood tree the day before came back to her, the lost look in the old woman's eyes, her clothes filthy, and the leaves and dirt in her hair. And then the story she'd told, the story she'd now told both of them.

"This is our fault, isn't it?" Estrella asked.

"I don't know, Estrella," Monica said, and there was a tired feel to her voice. "I don't know how it could be, really. All we did was ask some questions about our family. What I don't understand is why everything she says is so horrible. I don't want to hear them anymore. I want the Nana back who orders us around and is mean to us. I don't want this one." She dropped her arms and pushed away from the sink. "I've got to go. But do me a favor, Estrella. Whatever else Nana tells you, don't tell me."

Carmella Rael was lying on top of the blanket, her head propped on a pillow, her hands folded together on her stomach. She was wearing an old white nightgown that was buttoned at the neck and came to just below her knees. Her feet were bare. One of the two windows opposite the bed was open, and Estrella could smell the faint odor of manure from the Vargas corral across the road. She sat down on the edge of the bed and put her hand over the old woman's hands.

"Nana," she said. "How are you feeling?"

"Which one are you?" the old woman asked without turning her head. Her eyes were open, and Estrella wondered just how long she'd been lying in bed awake.

181

"I'm Estrella," she said. She moved her hand, and stroked her grandmother's hair lightly.

"You're the one who married that man who's not from the village."

"Yes, Nana," Estrella said, smiling a little. "I am."

The old woman turned her head slowly and looked at her granddaughter. "What my cousins did to me was bad enough," she said, "but what was worse was everyone thinking it was something I wanted. I don't even remember who I was before my cousins got to me. And it was our family who did that."

"I'm sorry, Nana," Estrella said, still stroking her hair. She felt like she was sitting with one of her daughters when they were sick and feverish. Stroking their hair and so worried for them that her chest would tighten and her throat would knot and she would need Will to sit with her. "I'm so sorry that happened to you, Nana." She realized it was what Will had said.

The old woman looked back up at the ceiling. "Where's Monica?" she said. "I don't feel so good."

"She went to work," Estrella said. "Maybe you should sleep for a little while. You might feel better then."

"I don't want to sleep. I have the rest of my life to sleep, don't you know? I remember when Lucida Munoz put her three children to sleep one night and not one of them ever woke up again. Oh sí, I remember that. She was your grandfather's second cousin and married one of those Quintana men from up north. They lived in a small house close to the church, and the only thing her husband was good for was drinking whiskey and beating his wife with his fists. It got so bad that their neighbors stopped seeing them, and when the priest led Mass in the summer, he would keep the doors of the church closed so his sermon would not be disturbed by the sounds she made when he struck her. I don't know why Lucinda chose to do that to her children, and even when she was old and her husband was long dead she never spoke of it. She lived with her brother, Eduardo was his name, who had the mind of a child and who froze to death one winter day walking to the village. Who knows what made him leave his house that morning. The snow was up to his waist, and no one can walk in snow like that, let alone a man who has a mind like a boy. When I told Monica that story, she began to cry. She tried to keep quiet with it, but my ears are still good. Where did Monica go, anyway?"

"She went to work, Nana," Estrella said. Somewhere along the way she had stopped stroking her grandmother's hair, and her hands were now clasped tightly in her lap. There was a hollow feeling in her stomach, and she wasn't sure whether it was from not eating that morning or from the story she'd just heard.

"She should be home with her children," Nana said.

"Her children are in school," Estrella said.

"And that man she married. He's good for nothing."

Estrella closed her eyes and shook her head. "I wanted to ask you something, Nana," she said, although, like her sister, she was unsure if she wanted to hear anything her grandmother had to say anymore. "I wanted to ask you about Manuela García."

"Manuela García," the old woman said. Her jaw was moving back and forth as if she was chewing on something. Her false teeth were in a glass on the table beside the bed, and her mouth was sunk in a little bit.

"Yes," Estrella said. "Manuela García. You told me there was something wrong with her. That she had secrets and Will should be careful working for her."

"I don't know Manuela García," the old woman said slowly. "I only know about her. But how could there not be." The old woman's hand lay on the bed beside her, and Estrella reached out and took it.

"I don't know what you mean, Nana," she said.

"She didn't have a mother," Carmella Rael said. "Her mother ran away from the village when Manuela was young and left her to be raised by men. I don't even remember her father's name. He was a big man, but whatever was once inside him was gone. He was empty, hija, as if his heart and soul had left one day, leaving not much of anything behind. I remember he sheared sheep and butchered cows and shoed horses. He did that kind of work. I remember he was killed while still a young man by one of Horacio Medina's horses. He was shoeing it when the animal kicked back and crushed in the side of his head. They said it happened so fast. One minute he was reaching for his hammer, and the next he was dead. But nobody much missed him. I don't think even Manuela García could miss a father like that. It would be like missing something that wasn't even there."

Estrella pressed her grandmother's hand gently. "You said she was raised by men. Who cared for her after her father's death?"

Carmella Rael's jaw moved by itself as she stared up at the ceiling. "Her grandfather cared for her," she said, finally. "Bolivar García was his name."

"And what happened to him?" Estrella asked.

"I think you're right, hija," Nana said, pulling her hand away. "I think if I sleep I might feel a little better."

"Nana," Estrella said.

The old woman turned her head and looked at her granddaughter. Her eyes were milky and rimmed with red. Her skin was pale and drawn. "What happened to him?" she said. "He was killed in the woods and hung from a tree by Ray Pacheco for what he did to those little boys."

From outside the open window, Estrella heard the neighbor's truck start up and the crunch of gravel beneath its tires. She heard the sudden squawk of a magpie, sharp and shrill. A slight breeze moved the curtain by the window and Estrella could feel it cool against her face.

"What little boys?" she asked in a whisper.

"I don't know what little boys," her grandmother said. "All I know is they weren't my little boys."

# FOURTEEN

✤ WILL SAWYER WAS SITTING IN THE SHADE on the front steps of Manuela García's house. He was hunched over a little, his arms on his knees, his head hanging down, smoking a cigarette. The door just behind him was open; there wasn't a sound coming from inside. His shirt was stretched tight across his back, and he didn't much care anymore about the dirt and straw digging into his skin. He didn't care about the chill he could feel on his bare arms. He didn't care that by now it must be almost mid-afternoon. In fact, he wasn't sure what he cared about.

"Help me to my room, hijo," Manuela García had said to him when she'd finally finished her story. "I'm tired. I need to rest for a little while."

Near the end of her talking, the old woman's voice had become so hoarse that she was speaking almost in a whisper. Her head had dipped low and her shoulders had curved inward so much that it made her body seem hollowed out inside her nightgown. Her hair hung thin and lank on each side of her face. She was looking down at her hands in her lap, and when he leaned over the table and spoke her name, she didn't answer.

Will pushed his chair back, the scraping sound loud in the room, and stood up. His knees and back ached from sitting so long, and he found himself limping a little as he walked to the other side of the table. He put a hand on her shoulder. The bone there was hard and thin beneath his palm. He bent down closer to her and caught the scent of old clothes mixed with something sweet, like burnt sugar.

"Manuela," he said. "Let me help you stand up."

A soft humming sound came from her mouth, and then she moved slightly and looked up at him. Her eyes were dulled and bloodshot and there was an ashen look to her skin. "Close the curtains for me, hijo," she whispered, "before we go. I don't leave them open." She brought a hand up and placed it over his. "Go do it now, hijo," and then, again, she lowered her head.

Will pulled his hand away and straightened up. Across the room the carved figure of the boy stood off to one side of the windowsill, and outside the day was still in full sun. Will felt as if he'd been in this house for hours and was a little surprised it wasn't later than it was. He went over to the sink and, instead of pulling the curtains closed, stood there for a moment looking up the hill at the old house.

The ropes hanging down from the piñon tree were dead still. All three windows on the south wall were wide open. A faint shimmer of heat rose from the pile of trash that Will figured was from the damp clothes that lay at the bottom of it all. If it wasn't for the bones of two children he'd found buried in the wall, he thought, the place would be just like any of the other abandoned adobes scattered around the village. Some old, deserted house full of forgotten secrets where people had once lived.

I was in that house, he thought. And all I found were bones. There's no boy wandering through those rooms. I would have seen him. I would have heard him. I'm getting stuck in some old woman's imagination.

Then Leonardo Martinez, with his thick glasses and his yellowed fingers and his false teeth, pushed his way into the front of Will's mind, the old man sitting in the cab of his pickup on a wooded hillside miles north of the village.

"Did you know I was a twin?" he'd said. And when Will had turned, the old man had told him about losing Benito on a summer night that was like any other. And when the old man was done with his story, he'd stared away at nothing and said, "After all these years, I still look for him. Sometimes, I think I see him out in a field or in the weeds along a ditch. And when that happens, he's still a little boy, and I'm an old man. I don't know how that can be, do you?"

"No," Will said now beneath his breath in the kitchen of Manuela García's house more than thirty years later. "I don't know how that can be."

From behind him, he heard Manuela García stir in her chair. "Close the curtains, hijo," she said, softly, "and help me to my bed."

Will stood where he was for a few more seconds gazing out at the old house. Then, shaking his head, he reached out and drew the curtains closed.

Will was smoking his second cigarette when Felipe's pickup turned into Manuela García's drive. He watched Felipe park beside his truck. Then the pickup door swung open and Felipe got out. He took a few steps toward the house and then stopped and threw both his arms up in the air.

Will took one more hit off his cigarette and flicked it away. He stood up slowly and took a second to stretch out his back. He glanced over his shoulder into the house, and then walked over to where Felipe was waiting.

"Hey," he said.

"Hey, yourself," Felipe said. "I thought you were quitting

this job, and here I find you sitting on the steps like you moved in." He kept his voice just above a harsh whisper. The last thing he wanted was for that old woman to come outside and give him a hard time again. He looked past Will at the house. "Where is she?"

"She's inside," Will said, holding up a hand and then letting it fall. "She's resting. What are you doing here, anyway?"

Felipe brought his eyes back to Will. "Looking for you," he said. "What do you think I'm doing? Estrella told me you were over here."

After leaving Flavio Montoya's house, Felipe had thought he could go home and be left in peace. But he'd only made it a half mile when he began to wonder, what if Flavio wasn't the only viejo in Guadalupe who'd lost a relative over the last fifty years. For all he knew, half the damn village might have not only lost somebody but had heard the story that jodido Eli Ortega was spreading all over the place. He pictured Elena standing outside the door of their house, her arms crossed, that look on her face, with a list of names in her hand of one old man after another that she wanted him to talk to.

So instead of taking the turn to his house, he'd driven over to the lumberyard to ask if anyone had seen Will. After that, he'd cruised the village looking for his truck until finally ending up at Will's place where Estrella had told him that Will had gone to work that morning at Manuela García's house, and that if he saw him to tell him to come home.

And she hadn't looked too happy, either, Felipe remembered but didn't say. In fact, Estrella, who was always sweet and even-tempered around him, had looked tired and worried and upset. About what, he didn't know and wasn't about to ask. His morning had been bad enough as it was.

"I came to tell you," Felipe said, "that I was at my neighbor's house. Flavio Montoya. You know him, he lives just down the hill from me. He's got this idea that those bones you found are his nephew's. I was there all morning with him. And let me tell you something, jodido, it wasn't much fun sitting with some old man who can only talk about sad things. But what was worse was thinking that if Flavio could believe things like this, maybe a bunch of other people in this village could, too. So, what I think you need to do is go over to the village office and talk to Donald Lucero about this. Tell him what you found and let him figure out who's buried in that old house. This is like one of those little things that can turn into a big deal if you're not careful." There, Felipe thought, taking in a lungful of air. He was a little out of breath from talking so long in a whisper. Now I can go home and tell Elena this is all straightened out.

Will had just stood there and listened while Felipe had gone on, and the longer he'd talked the more tired Will had felt. He didn't even bother to ask how Flavio Montoya had come to hear about this. He had a pretty good idea how that had happened and knew it wasn't worth bringing up. He raised his hands and ran them hard over his face and through his hair.

"So," he said, dropping his arms, "that's why you came here? To tell me that I should talk to Donald Lucero?" Ray Pacheco and a young Donald Lucero were the two Guadalupe police officers when Will had first come to the valley. After Ray Pacheco had died, Donald Lucero had pretty much taken over. Will had never cared for him. Somehow, he reminded Will of those men he'd known growing up, men from nearby ramshackle farms who seemed to have become like the land around them, flat and hard and gray and empty. Each one of them the kind of man his father had turned into.

Will looked beyond the cottonwood trees, at the field across the road that belonged to Bernabe Medina. It had been so dry for so long that there hadn't been enough alfalfa for even one cutting. All that was out there was a few stunted plants and scattered weeds and cracked dirt.

"That's why I left there," Will said, almost to himself. "So I could stay away from men like that."

"Left where?" Felipe asked, suddenly confused. "What are you talking about, jodido?" And then, like he'd been blind all this time, he noticed how dirty Will's clothes were. He saw the bits of straw in Will's hair and the dirt streaked on his neck where sweat had run. His hands were filthy and beat up. Felipe could see where two of Will's knuckles were torn and bloodied. Of course, he thought, that jodido's been digging in that old house again, and though he was standing in full sun, he felt a chill run through him, as if he was in some cold place. He reached out and touched Will's arm.

"Are you okay?" he asked.

Will turned his head and looked back at Felipe. He almost smiled. "Yeah," he said. "I'm okay. I've just been here too long." He cupped his hands and lit yet another cigarette, and blew the smoke off to the side.

"I found another one," he said.

Felipe opened his mouth and then closed it. Then, forgetting all about whispering, he said, "Another what?" although he had a bad feeling that he knew exactly what Will was talking about.

"Another set of bones," Will said. "In the same wall. And you know what? I think there's more up there."

Even though Felipe had heard each word Will had just said, it was his grandmother's voice that came out of nowhere and pushed its way into his head. His abuela, her red, swollen hands messing with those dried-up apple dolls that he never liked, telling him the dead were buried everywhere in this village. And if he knew what was good for him, he would never ever go near Patricio Martinez's chicken coop. He wondered now why she hadn't told him about the old García house. Then it struck him that just about every problem he had at this moment was because of women. From his grandmother to Elena to that old woman asleep inside the house to his youngest granddaughter who never listened and liked to throw things at him.

"So, there's two up there," he said, not knowing what else to say.

"Yes," Will said. "There's two. At least for now there's two. I don't know much, but I know this whole mess is twisted up with the old man who used to live there. Bolivar García. He was Manuela's grandfather." He thought it best not to get into what Manuela had said about being undressed by the old man. He knew there was only so much Felipe could take.

Felipe looked up the hill at the old house, at the sagging, twisted windows, at the pile of trash, at the swaybacked roof that looked like it wanted to fall in. In his mind, he could picture a gaping hole that Will had made in the wall with the skeletons of two children inside it. He let out a long, slow breath.

"I don't even know a Bolivar García," he said, looking back at Will. "I never even heard of a Bolivar García. So, what did she say when you told her. You told her, right?"

"Yes," Will said. "I told her."

"So, what did she say, jodido?"

Will took a long hit off his cigarette and blew the smoke slowly out of his lungs. "You sure you want to know?" he asked.

For a second, Felipe didn't say a word. Will was smiling just a little, and all Felipe could think was how could anything be worse than what he'd already heard. Even so, he still felt a slight misgiving as he said, "Eee, hombre, just tell me, would you?"

It took some work to get Manuela García out of her chair in the kitchen. The first time she tried to stand, her legs gave way and she sank down so quickly that Will had to grab her shoulders or she would have fallen to the floor. The second time she tried wasn't much better. Then she just sat there, her head bent, her hands in her lap, her skin bone white.

"Manuela," Will said, standing beside her. He'd never before glimpsed one bit of weakness in her and was suddenly afraid that this might be more than just being tired. "Let me carry you."

"No," she said sharply, and her voice was all air. "I don't want that. I'm not a child."

"All right," he said. "I'll just help you then." He crouched down and slid his hand between her arm and her ribs and around her back. "We're going to stand now," he said, and he raised her to her feet slowly. Her breath was harsh and ragged, and she was so light that Will wondered when she had last eaten. He slid the chair out of the way with his foot, and carefully he guided her out of the kitchen, down the hallway, to her bedroom.

Will eased her down on the edge of the bed, and she managed without his help to raise one leg and then the other onto the mattress. She lay down flat, her head on the pillow, her eyes looking up at the ceiling. The room was warm and lit with sunlight coming in the window. The bed had been made, and there was not one thing lying about. A bureau was set against one wall, and nothing was hanging on the walls.

"I'm cold, hijo," the old woman said.

Will walked around the bed. He pulled the quilt loose and covered her with it. "There," he said. "Do you need anything else?"

"No," Manuela said, looking at him.

"Then I should go."

The old woman stretched out her arm and took his hand, pulling him closer to the bed. "I want to tell you," she said, "that I played a part in all this, but I don't know what it is. I don't know what I could have done different. All I know is that I can't go up to my grandfather's house again. I can't bear it. Do you understand?"

"No," Will said, and pulled his hand away. "I don't understand."

The old woman grunted softly and closed her eyes. She pulled her hand beneath the quilt. "Have you listened to nothing?" she asked him, and now there was an edge to her voice. "I want you to go to my grandfather's house. The boy's not waiting for me anymore, Will. He's waiting for you." She turned her face away. "Now go," she said, "and let me rest."

While telling all this to Felipe, Will had walked over to his truck and was now leaning back against the tailgate. He'd stepped out his cigarette a while ago, and his hands were in his pockets. He felt a little better after telling Felipe what had happened that morning with Manuela García, but not much. "So, what do you think?" he asked.

Felipe had absolutely no idea what he thought, other than he was glad he wasn't Will. On top of that, even though he was sick of old women, he found himself once again thinking of his grandmother. He thought that she would have loved Will's story, a story full of dead bodies and crazy people and old houses and the ghosts of little boys. It was a story she might have enjoyed telling him on one of those dark, winter days when his mother would make him walk through the snow to her house with a paper bag full of fresh tortillas and tamales. While he sat by her stove to get warm, his grandmother would have given him one of her ugly apple dolls to hold and then said, "Did I ever tell you, hijo, about Manuela García and her grandfather, Bolivar García, and the dead children they kept in their house?" Then she would have leaned so close to him that he could have smelled garlic and something he didn't know on her breath. "Not everything dies, Felipe. Some things stay around for little boys like you to find them."

Now, Felipe glanced up the hill at the old house and then looked quickly away at the foothills. "This is like one of those old stories my grandmother used to tell to scare me," he said. Then he looked at Will, who was staring back at him. He shook his head back and forth slowly. "How do you get in these messes, anyway?" he asked.

Will smiled and straightened up. "So, you think it's my fault someone buried children in that house?"

"I didn't say that, jodido," Felipe said, although it occurred to him that life, especially his own, was far simpler when he only knew a little bit about things. And right now, he knew far more than he wanted. "So, what are you going to do?"

"I'm going home," Will said, "to drink a beer and talk to Estrella."

"What about Donald Lucero?"

"What about him?"

"Eee, are you going to talk to him?"

"I already heard he's looking for me," Will said. "Pepe at the café told me. But you know what? I don't like Donald Lucero."

"So?" Felipe said. "Nobody likes him. That doesn't mean you shouldn't go talk to him."

"I'll think about it," Will said, and walked to the door of his truck. Far off to the west, he could see a low bank of clouds. He wondered where they had come from. He couldn't remember the last time he'd seen clouds that might bring rain. He pulled the truck door open and then looked over at Manuela García's house, at the shadows just inside the open door.

She's still sleeping, he thought, or maybe lying awake staring at nothing. He glanced over at Felipe. "I'll give you a call later," he said. "Come on, let's get out of here."

# FIFTEEN

⚘ **THE SOUND OF RAIN** woke Manuela García from her sleep—rain and the distant, low rumble of thunder. The light in her bedroom had grown dim and gray. She could hear the steady drip of water running from the eaves of her roof. Will had left the door to the house open, and the air inside felt damp and smelled of wet dirt. Even though she was still covered with the quilt, her arms and legs and feet were cold. Manuela shifted onto her side, drew her legs up, and looked out the window.

Where did this rain come from? she wondered. Out the window, she could see that the leaves on the cottonwoods were dripping wet, and that low, heavy clouds filled the sky. How could things change so quickly? When I laid down my room was all sun.

She still felt tired and drained. There was a dull pain in the center of her back that ran up through her neck to the base of her skull. The muscles in her calves were aching, as if she had walked miles in her sleep. She was cold, too. A flat, empty chill that made it seem as if there was no warmth beneath the quilt. She knew without seeing that Will's truck was gone.

He's gone back to his family, she thought, to his little girls and that wife of his. Or maybe to drink whiskey with the other men in the village. In her mind she saw him walking down the hill from her grandfather's house. She remembered how slow he'd walked, how his head was bent, his shoulders slouched, how he dragged the shovel behind him. And she knew then, even if he didn't, that he would be back. He had come too far into this not to come back. And that thought almost made her smile.

Manuela watched as a sudden breeze moved the leaves on the cottonwood trees and water from the eaves blew against the glass. She heard the door to the house creak and then slam shut. She felt her heart begin to pound in her chest, and she waited to hear his footsteps in the hallway, his hand on the doorknob, to feel his hand on her clothes, his hand, calloused and filthy, on her body. And no matter how many times that had happened, no matter how old she had been, each time had been like the first, when the shock of it had made her feel she was becoming both more and less of what she was.

"Mi hija," he would say afterwards, petting her. And even after he was gone, she would hear his voice, as if it had become part of her.

"You're dead," Manuela whispered now. "And I'm so old that even you wouldn't want me."

Ray Pacheco had stood there, looking up the hill at the old house. In his hands, he held her grandfather's coat and the things that had been found in his pockets, coins and polished stones and a few marbles.

"Your grandfather, Bolivar García, is dead," he had said without looking at her. He looked older than he had just the week before when he'd come by asking about her grandfather. The skin beneath his eyes was dark and swollen, and there was a yellow caste to his skin. His hair, which she remembered being black, was now streaked with gray.

"I found him with a boy," he told her.

"I don't want to hear that," Manuela had said. She was wearing a thin white dress, and her feet were bare. Her hair hung down long.

"It was one of the Vargas boys. Renato is his name. He's nine years old. Just a little boy. I found them in the woods by the creek."

"You should leave now," Manuela had said, looking away from him. "Leave his things outside. I don't want them in my house." Then she turned and went inside, leaving Ray Pacheco to himself.

Years and years later, Manuela heard that Ray Pacheco, who was an old man by then, had shot himself near the edge of the river and then lain there alone in the sagebrush for so long that the crows got at him. The story she'd been told was that he'd been sick for a long time and had decided to spare his family and end his life. Manuela didn't give it much thought. After all, they had only known each other for a brief time, and even if they had shared something, that had been decades before. But the few times Ray Pacheco crossed her mind, she wondered if that day in the woods had followed him through his life all the way to the edge of the river.

All our stories are coming to an end, Manuela thought now. Even my own. She rolled over onto her back and then, groaning a little at the ache behind her heart, threw off the quilt and sat up slowly. She sat for a moment, her head lowered, her hair hanging down, her breath shallow. The pain in her calves had eased somewhat, and she swung her legs off the bed. She stood up carefully and made her way, one step at a time, out of the bedroom to the front door.

It was cold in the house. Manuela pulled her sweater tight across her chest and held it there with one hand. The rain seemed to be falling even harder now. Water was pooled in the ruts of the drive, and the floor just inside the door was wet.

She could feel the dampness in the air, and a deep chill ran through her. Once again, she heard the low sound of thunder. Like some animal had come to the valley, she thought. And then she reached out and swung the door closed.

It was dark in the kitchen. Manuela stood just inside the doorway, leaning against the edge of the frame. It had taken her a while to walk through her house, having to rest every so often to catch her breath. She could hear the steady rainfall. She could see that the chair she had sat on earlier was pushed away from the table, and that all of her counters were clean, everything put away except for the coffee cup Will had drunk from.

She walked across the room to the sink and, still holding her sweater closed with one hand, reached out and pulled the curtains open. The boy stood on one corner of the sill up against the glass.

"I'm sorry," Manuela whispered, "that I left you here." She had to stretch to reach him, and she felt the ache in her legs start up again. "Come with me," she said, holding him, and then went to the table and sat down.

The glass in the window above the sink was streaked with water, and the world beyond it was all gray. The air was full of water, and the foothills were covered with a thick layer of clouds. The sagebrush had been leeched of color and was wet and dark and huddled within itself. Even the piñon tree, with its hanging ropes, looked gray and old, as if it had stood alone up on that hill for too long.

The windows to the old house hung open. The walls were stained dark from rain. A bit of mist, like smoke, rose from the boards on the roof. The pile of Bolivar García's possessions that lay just outside the south door had sunk down with the moisture and looked small and drab and worthless.

Manuela leaned back in her chair. The boy was in her hands in her lap. Her sweater had pulled apart. She felt warmer now.

Her knees were slightly apart, and the ache in her muscles was gone. Her breath came so slight she was barely breathing. Every so often, a sharp pain would move through her back, touch her heart, and then leave.

I could sleep again, Manuela thought to herself, and at that moment the rain outside thickened and turned to snow. Manuela watched as the wind picked up and snow blew against the window. It began to fall even harder, so hard that all she could see of her grandfather's house was a dim light that moved from room to room. And then she heard the front door open and the sound of footsteps walking toward her. And a moment later, her mother walked into the room.

"Mi hija," Josefina said, kneeling beside her daughter's chair. Her hair was black and wet from the snow. Her shirt was torn at the neck, and that, too, was wet and clung to her body. Water ran from her dress to the floor. She smiled and touched the side of Manuela's face. "I told you I would be gone for only a little while," she said.

Manuela breathed in a shuddering breath. "You were gone so long," she said. "You were gone so long."

Josefina pulled her daughter's face to her and kissed her on the lips.

Manuela felt a great pressure rise in her chest. It filled her throat. "I never cry," she said. "I never cried, mama."

"I know you didn't, my love," her mother said.

# SIXTEEN

꘎ "IT'S SNOWING," WILL SAID. He was standing just inside the door of his house. A few hours ago, the sun had been out and it had been warm, and then the clouds he had seen earlier from Manuela García's steps had filled the valley. And soon after that, it had begun to rain. A cold, hard rain that filled the ditches and turned everything to mud. And now the temperature had dropped so much it had turned to snow. He knew it wouldn't amount to much. It was melting almost as fast as it fell, and what stayed would be gone after an hour of sun. But still, it was the first snow of the year. He felt Estrella come up behind him. She wrapped her arms around his belly and leaned her cheek against his shoulder. He could smell the whiskey on her breath.

"I should call Monica," she said, "and make sure the girls see this." She felt a rush of sadness grab at her heart. It was the first snow of the year, and her girls were not with her. As soon as Ella and Emilia had gotten home from school, she had loaded them into her pickup and taken them to Monica's house. When they'd asked why, Estrella hadn't known what to say other than, "I don't know why, you just are," and the lie made her feel even worse.

Monica had taken one look at Estrella, shaken her head, and chased all the kids outside. She closed the door behind them, and turned to her sister. "What's wrong?" she said. She couldn't remember the last time she'd seen Estrella this upset, and the first thought that she had was that something bad had happened to Will.

"It's Nana," Estrella said, her voice tight and strained. "What she told me."

Monica stared across the room at her sister. Estrella's hair hadn't been brushed, and her blouse was tucked in on only one side. Her eyes were red, and Monica could see faint lines running across her forehead that she had never noticed before. She closed her eyes and wondered what horrible story had come out of their grandmother's mouth now.

Monica took in a deep breath and eased it out slowly. Okay, she thought. Then she put her hands on Estrella's shoulders and steered her to a chair at the kitchen table. She went to the cabinet above the counter and got out two glasses and the bottle of whiskey Lawrence sometimes sipped from. She brought it all to the table and poured a little in each glass. She sat down across from Estrella.

"All right," Monica said. "What did she tell you now?"

It took Estrella some time to tell Monica the story. Every so often she would get mixed up in the telling of it and would have to backtrack from Will to Nana to Manuela García to the old woman's grandfather to Ray Pacheco, like the whole thing didn't even have a beginning but was some twisted circle that went everywhere. By the time she was done, her whiskey was gone, her face was flushed, and she had almost confused herself. On top of that, she was tired and felt like crying and didn't know if it was from worrying all day or drinking so much whiskey or both. She leaned forward and poured a little more in her glass.

As Estrella had gone on, Monica found herself thinking that her sister reminded her of her own children when they woke at night from a bad dream. She would hear them cry out and then rush to their room. There she would sit with them and stroke their backs with her fingers, telling each one not to cry, that they were safe now, and that what they had dreamed wasn't real. And after a while, their breath would deepen and they would fall back asleep.

After leaving her grandmother's house that morning, Monica had driven straight to work. It had been quiet at the village office, and for most of the morning she'd sat at her desk in a miserable mood. Sometime after lunch, while staring absently out a window at two horses who seemed to be staring back at her from a field across the road, it occurred to her that her grandmother had always told her and Estrella horrible stories, even when they were little. There were stories about her neighbors who buried dead chickens around her house at night, or how the Guadalupe cemetery would sometimes burn for no reason, or how the first man to ever walk into this valley lost his mind from loneliness and lived for years like a wild animal. She remembered another one about some black man who appeared in the village out of nowhere and, when not roaming the foothills, would peer into children's windows when they were sleeping. And then, of course, there was Rufino Trujillo, who Nana said had come back from the dead as an owl and lived in her apple tree. She didn't even want to think about what her grandmother had told her would happen on her wedding night, which, thankfully, didn't. Monica realized then that the mistake she and Estrella had made wasn't in listening to their Nana's stories, but in believing them. After all, how many bad things could happen in one family? How many bad things could really happen in a village as small as Guadalupe?

"Estrella," Monica said, leaning forward over her kitchen table. "They're just stories Nana told us. They're not true. She likes doing this to us. It's like we're little again and she wants to scare us."

From outside, Estrella could hear the voices of all five children yelling about something, and then that faded slowly as they ran to the far side of the house. Out the window in the opposite wall, she could see the foothills rising out of the valley and, beyond them, the rounded peaks of the mountains. Although the canyons that sliced through them were shadowed, the slopes were in full sun. She moved her eyes back to her sister.

"But Will told me he found the body of a child," she said. "And then what Nana said."

Monica shrugged her shoulders. "I'm sure he found something," she said. "And we both know Nana will say anything. But you're going too far with all this. I bet you anything Manuela told him a whole different story, and now he's out drinking a beer with Felipe. Either that or he's home waiting for you."

Estrella looked down at the table. She wanted to believe what her sister said, but she remembered the look on her grandmother's face earlier that day. It wasn't the look of someone who wanted to tell a scary story. It was the look of someone who didn't want to remember it. "I don't know," she said slowly. "Monica, I don't know."

"Well I do," Monica said. "So this is what we'll do. Leave the kids here tonight. I'll make sure they get to school in the morning. You go home and talk to Will. If he's not there, then call me." She pushed her chair back and stood up. At that moment, a cloud covered the sun and the room darkened.

"Even if everything Nana said was true," Monica went on, smiling a little, "it's not our story, Estrella. It's someone else's. It doesn't have anything to do with us."

"It's cold, Will," Estrella said, pressing her body tight against him. "Close the door." She was so tired and, for whatever reason, the sight of the snow falling made her want to cry again. It's the whiskey, she thought. But still, she felt as though the chill in the house was burrowing beneath her skin to her heart.

By the time Will had gotten home from Manuela García's place late that afternoon, it had begun to rain lightly, a soft, steady drizzle that he knew was going to get worse. He unloaded the tools from the back of the pickup and then went inside the house and made a pot of coffee. When it was done, he poured a cup, dragged a chair over to the open door and sat down and lit a cigarette. The sky outside was a dull gray, and there was no wind. From far away came the low sound of thunder without lightning. He wondered where Estrella and the girls were and then pushed the thought away, thinking that wherever they were they'd be home soon enough. He stretched out his legs and crossed them at the ankles, took a hit off his cigarette, and watched as the cloud of smoke was taken by the rain. He tossed the butt out the door, folded his hands, and closed his eyes. A soft breeze pushed a mist of water against his face.

Will thought about what that old woman had said about the boy in her grandfather's house. In fact, that was about all he could think about. And he knew he would have trouble sharing it with anyone, with Felipe, with Joe Vigil, with Estrella. Really the only person he could share it with, who might actually believe it, was long dead.

"Oh sí, viejo," he whispered, his head a little lower now. "I still remember."

207

After that day on the hillside thirty years ago, Will never spoke to Leonardo Martinez again. He caught sight of him now and again driving slowly on the edge of the highway and noticed his truck parked outside of Felix's Cafe or at the lumberyard or at Tito's Bar. But that was about it. The few times their eyes did meet, Leonardo had looked away as if he'd forgotten that the two of them had once shared time together on an empty hillside miles north of the village.

Only a few months after they met, Will heard that the old man had died. The story was that he had been found in the cab of his pickup, parked just off the road at the edge of an alfalfa field. Tito Chacon told everyone later that, other than the old man's eyes being open, he hadn't looked much different than when he was alive. He'd even had a cigarette stuck between two fingers. Tito went on to say that if he had one wish it would be to leave this life the way Leonardo had, looking out at a green alfalfa field and beyond to the high mountains to the east.

Will didn't say anything when he heard that, but he'd wondered just what it was the old man had last seen before he died. He wondered if it was like Tito had said, or if Leonardo hadn't even noticed the mountains but was gazing at a small boy standing alone in the middle of the alfalfa field.

As for the job he and Leonardo had looked at, it never happened. The owner called and told Will that he'd decided the place was too far away from everything, and that was that. When Will thought of that afternoon on the hillside, which was hardly ever, or at least not until Manuela García had wandered into his life, he could see in his mind the small clearing of scrub oak and the tracks their two trucks had left in the soft dirt, and the small pile of scattered cigarette butts the old man had smoked while he told the story about his brother Benito.

"Will," Estrella said again. "Close the door. I'm so cold." It was nearly dark out now and all she really wanted was to drag Will to the bedroom, lie down close to him, and sleep. "Will," she said again.

"Yes," he answered. "I know." He swung the door shut. Then he turned and put his arms around her waist. He brought his hands up her back, to her shoulders, and pulled her close. "I should shower," he said.

And this he only thought: I should tell you what happened today.

"No," Estrella said. She could smell dirt and sweat on his skin, on his clothes. All she wanted right now was to lie with him. "I don't care. We can talk about everything in the morning." She pulled away and took his hand.

"Come, Will," she said. "Take me to bed."

# SEVENTEEN

**It was still raining** when Will woke the next morning. He could hear it falling on the metal roof and could hear water dripping from the eaves. Estrella lay close beside him, her hair thrown back on her pillow. She had one arm across his chest and was breathing the deep breath of sleep. Will could still smell the scent of whiskey.

Just before sleep the night before, she had turned into him. She had put her head on his shoulders, her arm across his body, her leg over his, and said, "I want to leave here, Will." The bedroom was so dark he couldn't see her face, and her words were a little slurred. "I want to be somewhere else," she said.

Staring straight up into the darkness, he threaded his fingers through her hair. "Why?" he asked.

"There's too much here. I want the girls to be somewhere where it's not like that."

It took a long time for Will to say anything. But when he did, he asked her, "Did you ever know an old man named Leonardo Martinez? You might have been too young to remember him, but we got to know each other one day a long time ago." But Estrella was already asleep.

It was warm beneath the blankets, and he wanted to stay there. Although his sleep had been deep and heavy, he was still tired. An ache low in his back stretched into one hip from the digging he'd done the day before. The two fingers he'd scraped on his right hand felt tight and swollen. He turned his head and looked out the window.

It hadn't been light for very long. All Will could see outside were gray clouds and a light haze of low-hanging mist. He could feel Estrella's breath soft on his shoulder. And then he closed his eyes as Manuela García crept into his mind. He wondered if she, too, was lying in bed listening to the rain, or if she was sitting in the kitchen in the dark, sitting there by herself, staring out the window, waiting for him to come.

This is crazy, he thought. I don't even know what's real. And then, as if through her eyes, he saw the old house up on the hill. The rain dripping through the rotted boards of the roof, the open windows moving slightly back and forth, as if breathing. Rain water, too, would be running down the wall where he'd found the two small bodies. And somewhere in those three rooms, cold and shivering, was the boy Manuela thought she'd seen.

Carefully, Will moved Estrella's arm off his body. She moaned a little and spoke his name, and he stroked her hair until she quieted. Then he slid out of the bed. He gathered his clothes from the chair and left the bedroom.

He dressed in the kitchen in the dark while the coffee brewed. When it was done, he filled a glass jar with coffee, threw on a coat, and went into his daughters' bedroom. He sat down on the edge of Ella's bed and tore a page out of the notebook on the table beside it. He picked up a pen, and wrote,

*Estrella,*

*I hope you sleep late. Had to go, but I promise*

*I'll be home soon.*

*I love you.*

Will left the note on the kitchen table and, with one last look around the room, walked out of his life and into the rain.

The cottonwoods that lined the ditches along the back road were wet and sodden, their branches sagging heavy with moisture. The lights in all the houses were off, and every so often Will caught the thick odor of wood smoke from fires that had been started the night before. He had a cigarette going and sipped at his coffee. He drove slow, keeping out of the rain-filled potholes and away from the shoulder of the road where the mud might grab at his tires. The rain had eased up enough that he didn't need the wipers. He had the heater on in the truck and the window cracked, and every so often a chill would run through him.

He stopped where the road met the highway, where he could see around a little better. The mountains were buried in clouds. The foothills were dark and mist clung to them in places. The ditch that followed the highway was full with water. Sticks and weeds and plastic bags and empty cans ran along with it. Across the road, Eugenio Maestas's cows were huddled along the fence. They looked cold and sad.

Will turned left onto the highway and drove past Felix's Cafe. The lights were on and the lot outside was empty. He caught just a glimpse of Pepe and his father at a table in the back. He drove on by Tito's Bar and the lumberyard and, a mile or so farther, hung another left onto the road to Manuela García's house.

Bernabe Medina was outside when Will drove by. He was wearing a baseball hat and a heavy coat. The lights were all on in his house and the front door was open. He was standing by the pen where he kept his sheep, and though he didn't so much as glance Will's way, Will still raised a hand and said softly, "Hey, Bernabe." A moment later, the road ended at Manuela García's house.

If Will hadn't known better, he'd have thought the place had been abandoned. In this weather, the house looked dark and gray and neglected. It had begun to rain a little heavier now, and a sudden breeze sent a flurry of rain drops from the cottonwood trees down on his windshield. Buttoning up his coat, Will pushed open the truck door and climbed out of the cab. As always, he took a few seconds to bend over and stretch out the ache in his back, and then, hunched over from the damp, he walked to the house.

Without bothering to knock, he opened the door a crack and called out the old woman's name. When she didn't answer, he stepped inside. Her bedroom door was open. He glanced inside and saw that her bed was unmade and the room empty. He stood there for a moment, not quite sure what to do. The house was cold and smelled of old, damp clothes. He looked down the hallway into the kitchen where he could see part of the table and the counter beyond it.

"Manuela," he called out again. "It's Will." He pulled the front door all the way open so there'd be a little more light. Then he walked through the house to the kitchen.

She was sitting at the table, her hands loose in her lap, her head bent, and at first Will thought she was sleeping. He said her name yet again, and when she didn't answer he went over to her. He put his hand on her shoulder and felt the coldness of her skin seeping through the fabric.

"Hey," he said, softly. And even though a part of him already knew, he shook her a little. Her hands shifted slightly in her lap and the hair that lay on her shoulder moved before her face. "Manuela," he said once more. And then he pulled his hand away.

He was still for a while, listening to the steady fall of rain, feeling the emptiness in the house, and having no idea what to do. He thought he should call someone but didn't know who that would be. She had no family. She had no friends. For all he knew, all she had was him, someone she'd met just a few days ago.

It was the sight of the santo lying on the floor near her feet that finally got Will to move. He bent over and picked it up. It weighed almost nothing, and he could see where the boy's face had been rubbed so smooth by Manuela's fingers that his features were disfigured. Two fingers on his right hand had broken off, and the wood there was scarred. He placed it in the old woman's lap and then walked to the far side of the table.

She was wearing the same clothes she'd had on the day before, the low-slung nightgown, the frayed sweater, and her feet were bare. Though her head was lowered, he could see her face through the strands of hair. Her eyes were closed, and he could see the faded scar that ran down her cheek from the edge of one eye. He wondered why she hadn't told him how that had happened. He remembered that first day they'd met, when she'd told him the lie that had been the beginning. Sitting in that same chair, her hands folded, her head tilted up and off a little to one side.

"I want you to make my grandfather's house look the way it once did," she had said. "I want you to make an old woman happy." Then she had smiled that tight, hard smile.

"Who were you, Manuela?" Will whispered now. He stared at her a bit longer and then walked over to the sink. The curtains were open, and he reached out, unlatched the window, and pushed it wide open. A rush of cold, damp air came into the room.

After Bernabe Medina was done swinging the gate open so his sheep could go out into the field, he said to them as they walked by, "Cuidado, all of you. There are mean dogs out there. Watch out for each other."

He'd heard Will drive by just a few minutes before, and it made him remember that he wanted to tell the man something he'd forgotten. He wanted to say that his wife, Pelimora, wanted Will to know he should stay away from the García house, that some things were best left alone to themselves. But Will's truck had headed down the road and disappeared into the cottonwoods. As soon as it was out of sight, he closed the gate to the pen and latched it. Rainwater had seeped through the collar of his coat, and he could feel it lying cold and wet on the back of his neck. He walked away from the pen, past his truck, and a little ways down the drive. Then he stopped and looked back at his house.

The lights were on inside and he'd left the door to the house wide open, things that Pelimora had always chided him about.

"When you leave a room, Bernabe, you leave things behind that don't want to be forgotten. Like light switches and doors—" Here she would pause and look at him seriously before going on. "And me," she would finish. "Do you think we all forget about you?"

"No, Pelimora," Bernabe said now, standing alone in the rain looking at his house. Looking at the open door and a shadow he thought he saw moving behind his bedroom window and the empty flower beds and the new roof that Will had put on just a few years before. "I don't think that."

Bernabe was careful walking down the road. The last thing he needed to do was slip on the mud and fall. Something in him might break, and then he'd lie in the rain waiting for someone to come. And since few people ever drove by his house, he might lie there for a long time.

The rain was falling harder now, and he was relieved when he finally came to where the cottonwood trees shielded him a little from the downpour. He could hear the raindrops pattering the leaves. He couldn't remember when he had last seen a rain like this. Sometimes in the summer there would be late afternoon showers, but it was almost never that he woke up to it. It might have been the year, he thought, when the three creeks overflowed their banks and washed Demecio Segura, and why he was out in the rain no one knew, all the way across the valley to Octaviana Esquibel's house. Octaviana had been standing at her kitchen window explaining to God that although she wanted rain she didn't want this much rain, when Demecio, cut and bleeding and half drowned and covered with mud and weeds, crawled gasping out of the creek. When she saw him, she thought that what she saw was either some bad trick God had played on her or something her mind had made up, and she went into her bedroom and lay down until whichever it was went away.

"Yes," Bernabe said. "That's the last time I remember a rain like this. When Demecio was washed away."

When he came to Will's truck, he leaned against it to catch his breath. Not far in front of him was Manuela García's house. The door was open and somehow he expected to see the platter of enchiladas he'd left decades before sitting just outside her door. He shook his head a little and felt cold rain run down his back.

No, he thought to himself, that was a long time ago I was here. When I was a young man. He moved his eyes from the doorway and looked over the house. Weeds were growing up along the wall. The plaster was cracked, and the shingles on the roof were curled and streaked black near the eaves. The windows were dark, and most of the paint on the frames had peeled away. He knew the rain and the clouds didn't help, but still the place looked shabby and rundown, as if little had been done to it over the years. He felt bad for a second, thinking that he should have come here now and again over the years to help his neighbor out.

"Do you think I would have let you come here by yourself, Bernabe?" he heard Pelimora say. "Do you think you even wanted to come to this house?" He heard the long sigh his wife would sometimes make, like a soft breeze moving through leaves. "Come home now, Bernabe," she said. "I'm waiting for you."

"Soon, Pelimora," he whispered, standing beneath the cottonwood tree. "I have something to do first," but he could feel whatever that was slipping away from him.

He pushed off of the truck and walked over to the house, up the steps, to the front door. There was just enough daylight inside for him to see all the way to the far end of the house. He could make out part of a table and a chair and, beyond that, the far wall. For a second, he wondered what he was doing here, why he had come. He wondered if he should knock or call out and what he would say if anyone answered. Water was dripping from the eaves, and as Bernabe turned his head away from it he saw the old house up on the hill and remembered that he had seen it once before long ago. He remembered that it was the house where Manuela García's grandfather, Bolivar García, had once lived. He remembered that back then the place had at least looked like a house. Now, all that was left of the roof was bare, blackened wood. He could see that the place was leaning badly and that the roofline sagged like it might fall in at any moment. As Bernabe stared at it, out of the corner of his eye, he caught sight of someone standing motionless in the rain, just before the doorway.

He felt a thread of fear run through him and then a deep chill, as if he were falling sick with fever. I've been here before, he thought. He remembered that the foothills back then, too, had been wet and dark, and the sky had been gray and heavy with clouds. He remembered that Manuela García had slipped and fallen in the mud and that when she fell her dress had risen high up her thighs and he'd seen the sudden white flash of her skin. He remembered that instead of going to help her, he had left, as if ashamed that he had seen too much. He took a small, shuffling step away from the open door. And then, from somewhere far away, he heard Pelimora call for him.

"Bernabe," her voice came. "You're too old now. And he's not even from this village. It's not your place, or his, Bernabe. Come home to me. Your poor sheep are out in this rain."

"My sheep," the old man muttered, and he jerked his head back a little, as if surprised at himself for forgetting something so important. "I almost forgot about my sheep." He turned his head and looked down the road he had just walked. "How did I even come to be here?" he wondered. Then, holding an arm out so as not to lose his balance, he took the steps down carefully. And without a glance back, he began to walk away from Manuela García's house,

"I'm coming, Pelimora," Bernabe said, his head bent, his shoulders hunched from the rain. "I'm coming."

"There's nothing in this place but bones," Will reassured himself. He had been standing for a while just outside the south door of the old house. He was wet and cold and muddy and felt almost foolish not only for walking up the hillside in weather like this, but for finding himself staring at the closed door like he was afraid to push it open, like there was some truth to the story Manuela García had told him.

I've been inside this house for the past three days, he thought, and all I've found in there was dead things and filth and trash that no one wants. He couldn't say he'd felt the presence of anything except rot and decay and neglect. Besides all that, the image of Manuela García slumped in her chair was vivid in his mind and he didn't feel so good about leaving her alone in her house. As if the woman hadn't been treated bad enough in her life, he had to do this to her now that she was dead.

The rain had slowed to a steady drizzle. Trails of mist clung to the foothills, and the mountains beyond were buried in clouds. The sagebrush was wet and beaten down, and he could see his breath. It seemed almost impossible to think that the morning before had been warm and bone dry, the whole valley caught up in drought. Now, everything was rain. He looked back at the door. A breeze must have blown it shut, he thought. The grains in the wood had swelled tight. The latch was corroded with rust. From the west side of the house, he heard the creak of one of the windows moving. Other than that, and the soft sound of the rain, everything was still and quiet.

Two things finally got Will to move. The first was the thought that if Estrella wasn't already up, she would be soon, and he knew she would worry when she found him gone. The second was that of all the things that old woman had wanted from him, this was the last of it.

"My grandfather's house is one more story for you to have," she had said, not even bothering to ask if that was something he wanted. Or maybe she had, Will thought, and I didn't notice. He shook his head, and felt a thread of cold rain run from his hair down the back of his neck.

"What am I doing?" he muttered. "Standing in the rain like some old man. There's nothing in this fucking place but bones." Then he put the palm of his hand flat on the door and pushed it open.

The smell of wet mud and rotted boards and something else he couldn't quite recognize was so strong that he jerked his head and took a step back. Just inside, he could see puddles on the floor, and he could hear water dripping. Though light was coming in through the doorway and the open windows and the cracks in the roof, the house was still dim and murky, as if somehow the storm itself had crept inside the place. Will took in a deep breath and stepped inside.

Other than the water pooling in low spots on the floor and the rivulets running down the four walls, there was nothing in the first room that he hadn't seen before. He did notice that the adobe up high was so eroded that it wouldn't take many more storms before the wall caved in and the roof collapsed. A few years after that, all that would be left of the old García house would be rotted vigas and scattered glass. Will glanced toward the end of the house. Water was dripping throughout, and every so often he heard clumps of dirt fall from the ceiling. Then he stepped through the archway into the middle room.

The dirt he'd dug out of the wall the day before had flattened and turned to mud. Inside the hole he'd made, water was dripping from the cloth that held the second body. Not only were the bones beneath it wet, but the water had eaten away so much adobe that part of the arm was exposed. It looked as if whoever was in there was reaching out. And even though Will knew what he'd find there, the sight of it still sickened him. It made him want to cover the wall, as if their being seen this way was worse than what had happened to them.

Bad things happened here, he thought. And they happened to Manuela when she was a little girl. And they happened to Estrella's grandmother, and to who knows how many others behind closed doors and curtained windows, and in trees along creek beds, and out on empty mesas, and in old farmhouses a thousand miles away. They happened while people drank their beers and sipped their coffee and noticed nothing.

Will wondered if it was just a matter of luck who ended up in places like this and who didn't. He wondered what it meant for someone to take a walk on a summer evening and end up in a house like this. He stood staring at the remains of the two small children and listening to the water dripping through the roof until finally he turned and, dipping his head, went into the last room of the house.

There was standing water there, too, and the east door was wide open. The portal outside was sagging lower than he remembered, so low that all he could see outside was the slow rain falling on the pile of crosses and the flat lay of sagebrush beyond it. He circled the room, looking around at the four bare walls.

I'm in an empty house, he thought. There's nothing here. And if there ever was, it left a long time ago. Again, Manuela García went through his mind. He thought it was time to get out of here and go take care of that.

He went to the east door and pulled it closed. Then he walked over to the heavy cookstove. Large chunks of adobe had fallen on top of it and it was leaning forward a little from the weight. Both clawed legs were bent out at an angle, like the slot they slid into had broken. Will closed the two warming chamber doors on top and stooped over and shut the door to the oven. Lying on the floor near the base of the stove was another marble with almost the same markings as the one he'd given Ella a few days before. Will stared at it for a few seconds and then moved it with the side of his foot hard enough that it rolled beneath the stove. Shaking his head, he put a hand on the edge of the stove and went down on one knee. As he reached under the stove his foot slipped and the sudden weight of his body broke the legs loose and dropped the cookstove down on his wrist.

For one long second, Will didn't move. He didn't really feel any pain, just the sharp pressure of his hand caught tight between the packed floor and the lip on the stove. Then he tried to pull his hand free and felt the steel cut deep into his wrist.

That was when he got scared. Cursing, he swiveled onto both knees and tried to slide his hand sideways. When that didn't work, he dug into the dirt beneath his wrist with his free hand. It took only a minute for his fingernails to scrape against stone, and he realized the cookstove had been placed on a solid slab of rock. Again, he tried to pull his hand free and felt the steel dig deeper into his skin.

"Damn," he said. "I don't believe this." A dark thread of blood seeped from beneath the stove. He put his shoulder against the oven door and pushed up. The stove shifted ever so slightly, and then fell as both his knees slipped backwards on the wet dirt floor. And this time, though there was still no pain, he had a feeling that whatever had happened to his hand wasn't so good.

Will was smoking a cigarette that he had somehow managed to light with one hand. He brought it slowly to his mouth, inhaled, and then lowered his hand and let it rest easy on his thigh. His legs were stretched straight out and spread apart. The back of his head was resting against the oven door. A strip of cloth that he'd ripped from his shirt and tied around his arm just below his elbow had worked its way loose and slipped down his arm. He was tired from the struggle, and the bottom of his trousers were soaked through. He couldn't feel his hand, like it wasn't even there, and he had stopped looking at the amount of blood that had soaked into the floor beside him. The only good thing, he thought, was that the outside door to the room had swung open by itself and he was able to look out.

It was still raining, and from the angle he was sitting at he could see that mist was still hanging low on the base of the foothill. The pile of crosses just outside the door looked like nothing more than a rotted jumble of old wood and sticks and warped boards. The sagebrush was gray and stooped and wet.

He knew that the sky, if he'd been able to see it, would be thick and heavy with clouds.

Will remembered the years when it rained here, when the creeks would run high and storms would sit over the valley for days and the village would fall quiet and turn in on itself. He'd spent those years alone in his house looking out his open door at just about the same things he could see now. Those were the years before Estrella, before his daughters, the years when he felt nothing would ever change, when his whole life was gray and flat and his mind could wander through all of it without being bothered.

Will brought the cigarette to his mouth again and inhaled the sweet smoke. He let it ease out of his mouth slowly and watched it drift toward the open doorway. He wondered how much longer he'd have to sit here before someone came looking, and then, for some reason, he found that it didn't much matter to him, that it wasn't so bad sitting in this old house by himself. He let his head drop and closed his eyes. A wash of cool, damp air brushed across his face.

I could sleep, he thought. I could sleep for just a little while. And that's when he heard a noise—not of rain falling, or bits of adobe sliding loose, or the door swinging closed, but the shuffling sound of something moving.

He cracked open his eyes. Outside, rain was dripping from the portal roof, and inside, pockets of shadows filled the room. Will shifted his head slightly and out of the corner of his eye caught sight of a boy standing in the doorway between the rooms.

For a moment Will just stared at him, then he almost laughed. "So now you show up," Will said, and at that, without making a sound, the boy began to cry.

He cried with his arms wrapped around his belly, his face all twisted up. He was so skinny that Will could see each of his ribs. His hair was matted and too long and dark like his skin. He was wearing only a pair of underwear, and they were torn and grass stained. His chest was covered with a mesh of thin scratches. He looked sad and pathetic and reminded Will of Ella when she was little and had hurt herself and would cry until either he or Estrella sat and held her.

"Hey," Will said, and this time he spoke a little louder. "What are you doing here, anyway?" He wasn't sure why, but for as messed up as things were at this moment, he was happy to see the boy, as if he had stumbled upon something he'd lost a long time ago. It didn't matter that he wasn't quite sure just what he'd found.

"I got lost," the boy choked out. His nose was running, and he wiped at it with his arm. "I was with my brother and I got lost."

"I know you did," Will said, softly. "You got lost a long time ago, Benito."

Then Will was hit with a rush of fatigue so strong it made him dizzy. He moved his head and watched the rain out the open door until the feeling passed. After a moment, he glanced down at his hand. His cigarette had burned out. He spread his fingers and let it drop to the floor. With what strength he had, he put his hand down flat on the floor and pushed himself up straighter. Then he jerked the hand stuck beneath the cook-stove and, just like that, it pulled free.

"Jesus," he said. "That wasn't so hard." He held his hand in front of his face. Although the cut on his wrist looked deep, it had already begun to scar over and the blood on his fingers had dried. He flexed his hand carefully and it bent loose and easy at the wrist. Will wondered what Felipe would say about a hand that was mangled and bleeding one moment and healed the next, how that could ever happen.

"How should I know, jodido?" Felipe was a little out of breath, as if he had just come up the hill and walked into the house.

"Maybe God feels sorry for people like you," he said. "What I want to know is why you put your stupid hand beneath an old cookstove where spiders and centipedes live in the first place?"

"Something rolled under it," Will said, still looking at his hand, "and I tried to get it. How was I supposed to know the damn thing would fall over?"

"That's always been your problem, jodido," Felipe said. "You never know anything until it's too late."

He stepped in front of Will and squatted down. "Do you remember that time Juan Torres cut off his finger on that table saw we borrowed?"

"Yes," Will said, looking at Felipe. "I remember."

"Do you remember what you said?"

"No," Will said, although he did. "I remember about Rudy's dog, but I forgot what I said."

"Well, let me tell you then. You said, 'Does it hurt?' Juan just cut off his finger and all you got to say is does it hurt? That's like saying it might rain when it's raining." Felipe shook his head, sadly. "Sometimes I don't know about you."

Will remembered Juan letting out a yell and clutching his hand, and then everyone on the jobsite crowded around, looking at it and groaning. He remembered that Juan's finger had barely bled and that he stupidly asked Juan if it hurt. And he remembered Rudy's dog, one of those yapping dogs that was always underfoot and that no one liked, snatching the finger up in his jaws and sauntering off with it into the sagebrush like it was a leftover from somebody's lunch.

"What I want to know," Will said, getting a little angry, "is how come you only remember what I said and not what that dog did."

"Because this story's about you, not a dog." Felipe grunted and looked past Will. "I wonder what happened to that dog, anyway," he said. "I never even knew that dog's name."

"Rudy named him Chico because he was so little," Will said. "I got a feeling Chico didn't have one of those long lives."

"Oh sí, you're probably right. Juan probably snuck over to Rudy's house and shot him. I wouldn't want to live in the same village with a dog that ate part of me. But Rudy never had much luck with animals. Do you remember when his favorite pig tried to kill him?"

"Yes," Will said, smiling. "I remember that."

The two of them stopped talking then. Felipe was staring down at the floor, his tongue pushing out at his cheek where he'd had three teeth pulled a few years back. Will sat where he was, looking at him. He could see the deep lines running through Felipe's face and that his hair was mostly gray and how the skin at the corners of his eyes sagged. I've been in this village a long time, Will realized, long enough to watch the two of us get old.

Felipe raised his eyes and looked at Will. He jerked his head a little to one side. "What are you going to do about him?" he asked.

Will had almost forgotten about the boy and was a little surprised to see him still standing in the doorway between the two rooms. Benito had stopped crying and was just staring into the middle room. His arms were at his sides and Will could see a web of fine scars on his back. He wondered what had happened to the boy, and then didn't think about that anymore.

"You know what that kid's looking for, don't you?" Felipe asked.

"No," Will said, looking back at Felipe. "I have no idea what he's looking for."

"Oh sure, you don't," Felipe said, his voice not much more than a whisper. "What do you think happens when you're not here? Do you really think he's the only one in this old house?"

At that moment, the door at the far end of the house

227

slammed shut. The sound of it sent a deep chill through Will, and he felt the kind of dread he sometimes felt when his father had left him alone at night for too long. "That old man's dead," he whispered.

"So?" Felipe said. "Go ask my grandmother if dead things can hurt you. Go ask Manuela and see what she says. She's been telling you all along about dead things, but you didn't listen." He took in a deep breath and let it out slowly. "Come on, jodido," he said.

Then he took Will's hand and, as he stood, he pulled Will to his feet. He leaned close, so close that Will could smell garlic and stale beer on his breath. "Take him home, Will," Felipe said. "Get him out of here. It's too sad for him in this house. When you're done, come by and we'll drink a beer."

Will opened his mouth to speak and a hard, sudden wave of dizziness hit him. He leaned back against the cookstove, lowered his head, and gulped in air.

"Wait," he said, in between breaths. "I don't know if I can do this."

"I'm sorry, jodido, but you're on your own." And after a moment, he added, "You've always been on your own here," and now his voice was far away, like it had been carried off by a breeze. "I'll see you later."

When Will finally felt steady enough to raise his head, Felipe was gone. Other than the constant, slow drip of water, the house was dead still. Outside, the rain had stopped and the light had shifted as if it was growing dark. Will wondered how long he'd been in this old house. He looked over at the boy.

"Hey," Will said.

The boy's body spasmed like he was frightened, like no one had said a word to him in a long time, and he looked over his shoulder at Will. Then he turned around and took a slow step forward. "Can I come with you?" he asked.

The boy's voice seemed to be harsh and a little high at the same time. It struck Will that those were the same words Manuela García had heard almost eighty years before. He wondered how she had managed to leave this little boy behind and then realized not only that she'd had Bolivar García for a grandfather, but that she had been only nine years old.

I would have left him, too, he thought. I would have run away from this place and never come back.

Will pushed off the stove and stood there until he felt like he wouldn't topple over. "Yes," he breathed out. "You can come with me."

As he stepped toward Will, the boy said, "I have a twin brother. Did you know that?"

It was warm outside, warmer than it should have been. On top of that, there was no sign it had even rained. The ground was dry, the sky was clear, and the foothills were hazed a blood red. It felt to Will like a mid-summer evening, not late September, and he thought that he would think about how that could have happened later.

The man and the small boy angled slowly down the hill, picking their way through the sagebrush. Little by little, they moved away from the old house, away from Manuela García's place toward where the creek ran out of the foothills and flowed through the valley. For a while, Benito stayed close to Will and kept quiet. He walked along staring at the ground, his feet scuffing dirt like they were too heavy to lift. Maybe it was being out in the light, but the scratches and cuts on the boy's body seemed to have faded away. Once, when Benito began to cry, Will stopped walking. He put his hand on the boy's shoulder and knelt down in front of him.

"Are you okay?" he asked. Even though the creek was still a half mile away, Will could hear small birds there in the trees.

"Yes," Benito said. He wiped at his nose with his bare arms. "He took me."

"I know," Will said. "I'm sorry."

"That shouldn't have happened to me," the boy said. "It was bad."

"I know," Will said again, and now he saw not only Benito taken into that house, but his daughters and Felipe's grandchildren and every other child in the village. "I know it was bad. Your brother looked for you, did you know that? He looked for you everywhere."

"He should have found me then." The boy had been staring off at nothing, and now he looked at Will. "Did it make him sad?"

"Yes," Will said. "He was pretty sad."

"I kept thinking he would come. But then he didn't." He wiped at his nose again. "But Leonardo can't find anything. He's always losing things. He loses his glasses. He loses his socks. He loses my father's hammer. He even loses his marbles. I keep those so they don't get lost. I have to always look out for him."

The Leonardo that Will knew was a sad, old man with thick glasses and false teeth and an old pickup that spit out exhaust. He was an old man who smoked too much and died looking out at an alfalfa field. It was strange to hear Benito talk about his brother as a boy. It made Will feel not only as if time had gotten mixed up, but that his place in it had too. What was even more strange was how much of the story he already knew.

"That's not what I heard," he said, smiling a little. "I heard it's your brother who always looks out for you."

For a moment, the boy just stood still in front of Will, staring off, his mouth half open. Then his eyes grew wide and he grinned. "Did you hear about that dog that knocked me over?" and the words rushed out of his mouth. "I wasn't doing nothing at all, just walking along, and this dog comes running and sends me flying." He shrugged his shoulders and shook his head. "I don't know how dogs can run so quiet."

Will was beginning to think that if he'd known Felipe as a boy, he might have been like this. "I heard about that," he said. "I also heard he took your shoe."

"Dogs are stupid," Benito said. "There are sticks everywhere, and he wants my shoe. My mother wasn't so happy about that."

"I know a dog that ate somebody's finger."

"Eee," Benito breathed out. "I'd like to see that. Did you know that even though Leonardo was born first, I'm taller than he is?"

"Yes," Will said, standing up. "I knew that." It was darker now, and half a mile away the trees by the creek were in shadows.

"He was born first," Benito went on. His voice almost had a lilt to it now, "but my mother said that I was her greatest gift. That I was born when no one would have thought to look for me."

From nowhere, a wave of exhaustion struck Will. He felt lightheaded and wondered if it was from standing up too quickly. He thought he should sit down and rest for a little while, but then worried that he might never get up. He took a slow step forward. "Come on, Benito," he said. "It's going to be dark soon."

"We have to be careful by the creek," Benito said, following behind Will. "Victoria's little brother fell in and drowned."

"He fell in the ditch," Will said, not bothering to look back, paying attention to where he stepped. "Not the creek."

"I wonder how many fish are in the creek," Benito said. "I bet there's a hundred fish in the creek. I wonder what my father will say when me and Leonardo come home with a hundred fish."

It was cooler in the trees, though the creek was running low. The grass was high here and the branches from the juniper and piñon trees grabbed at Will's shirt. The ground was beginning to flatten out, and there were crickets and the whine of mosquitoes. They had walked about a half mile, winding slowly through the trees, when from not so far away there came the sound of an old woman yelling.

"That's old Mrs. García," Benito said. He was now about ten feet in front of Will. He'd found a stick and every so often would swing it at a branch that was in his way, or at nothing at all. "She was our midwife. She yells at everything. Papa says that if you're smart, you'll keep away from all those Garcías. He says those Garcías are nothing but trouble."

I remember all of this, Will thought. I remember every bit of it. That old woman's yelling for her son, who's an old man himself, to come inside and help her to bed. Then he heard the dull sound of a sledgehammer striking wood. A sharp sliver of fear dug into his heart and he began to breathe faster. He stopped walking and bent over, his hands on his knees. From nearby, he could hear the water in the creek moving over rocks. And from farther away came yet another sound. It was like a breeze pushing itself through the trees, and it carried the scent of old smoke and lard gone bad. Will realized that he and Benito were not the only ones in these woods and it made him feel as if he, too, was a small boy alone.

"Wait," Will said. "Come back here, Benito." The boy glanced back at him, and even in the growing dark Will could see he was on the verge of running off.

"No, Benito," Will said, again, and he could hear the harshness in his voice. "Please come back here." He watched as the boy took two steps away, and then, as if thinking better of it, ran to him.

"Eee," the boy said. "What happened to you?"

"Nothing," Will said. "I just needed to rest. You need to listen to me now."

"You know what's funny?" Benito said. "I don't remember where I put my clothes." He raised both arms and let them fall. "I think that dog took them."

"You left them by the creek," Will said. "You took them off so they wouldn't get wet. When you looked at the fish."

Benito stopped moving and stared at Will. For one long second, something dark and twisted crossed the boy's face, and then it was gone. It made Will think that this boy might always be haunted by something just beyond his reach.

"You can find your clothes later," Will said to him. "Tomorrow, you can find them." Again, he heard the sound of the sledgehammer hitting wood. He knew that if he were to walk out of the woods and into the road, he would see the lamp in the window Benito's mother had lit. He would see her standing at the sink in her kitchen, not yet worrying where her two boys were.

"Listen, Benito," Will went on, and he took the boy's arm. "I want you to stay with me now. We're going to walk together. You can't run ahead. You've got to promise me this."

"But I can get there fast fast. If I get there before Leonardo, I can hide and jump out at him."

Will closed his eyes. Not for the first time he was glad he had daughters. "No," he said. "You need to remember what your mother said. She said that you must always always be careful because at any moment something might happen. This is one of those times, Benito. You can scare your brother tomorrow. And when you see him," and here Will's voice broke. He shook his head. "And when you see him, I want you to run to him. And then both of you run as fast as you can to your father. Do you understand?"

"Yes," Benito said. "I can do that." From deeper in the woods, Will heard a mourning dove call. "We have to go now," he said.

"Who are you, anyway?" the boy said. "I never saw you before. Where are you from?"

Will shook his head. "I don't know where I'm from," he said. "I did once, but I don't anymore." He straightened up slowly and took Benito's hand and held it tight. "Come on," he said.

The trees were bigger here, junipers with sprawling limbs, the lower ones gray and dead, the piñons thick and heavy. Scrub oak and sagebrush were scattered about, and the ground was soft and covered with pine needles. From the far side of the creek, Will could hear something moving through the brush.

This story is coming to an end, he thought. He was still afraid, but he didn't know who for. He felt Benito pull on his hand.

"There," the boy said. "There's the path."

Just ahead was a small clearing by the creek. A path led to it. Then Will heard the voice of a small boy calling out Benito's name and a few seconds later saw the shadowed form of Leonardo Martinez. Will came to a dead stop.

"Hey," he whispered. "Hey, old man, I found you." He watched as the boy stopped walking and looked around. He had his arms wrapped around his stomach.

"Don't scare me, Benito," he called out, his voice wavering. "I don't want you to scare me."

"That's my brother!" Benito said. "That's Leonardo!"

"I know," Will said. He let go of Benito's hand. "Run, Benito," he said, and even as he went to push the boy forward, the boy was already gone.

"Leonardo!" Benito yelled, so loud that the woods fell still and whatever was in them was gone. "I found you, Leonardo!"

"Why did you leave me, Benito?" Leonardo yelled back. "I thought you got lost. I thought you would scare me. Eee, where are your clothes?"

"I don't know. I think that dog took them."

"How?"

"I don't know how. He just did."

"I thought you would scare me," Leonardo said again, and this time there were tears in his voice.

"I would never do that."

"What are you going to tell Mama about your clothes?"

"I don't know. I'll think of something." Benito glanced back into the woods and then looked at his brother. "Come, Leonardo, I'll race you home." And then the only sound was the sound of two boys running.

Will got lost not long after the boys ran off. He wandered through the woods on that warm summer evening, not exactly sure where he was or where he should go. One moment, he would feel a deep, searing need to see Estrella and his daughters, and the next he would remember Manuela García alone in her house. Then it would occur to him that having a cold beer with Felipe wouldn't be so bad. The only place he never wanted to see again was the old García house.

He followed the creek for a while, and then branched away from it toward the dirt road. It was a clear night, and Will could see a million stars. He could smell the thick scent of cut alfalfa and manure from Eugenio Maestas's field. He walked for a while, past the road that would have taken him home, past the lumberyard and Tito's Bar and Felix's Cafe. The village was dark and quiet. The only sound was the soft sound of water running through the ditches.

He walked until he came to the far edge of the valley and then went up the slope to where the hill crested. He was tired by now. His legs ached from walking, and the muscles in his back were tight and sore. There was an old ruin not far from the road and he sat near it, leaning back against the trunk of a long-dead piñon tree.

Below him, he could see how the valley was rimmed on all four sides by foothills, and beyond them to the east rose the high Sangre de Cristo Mountains. He could see the church and the cottonwood tree that grew beside it. He could see scattered old adobes and the fields of alfalfa. And as he gazed over this place that lay at the end of a long, long road, he thought that if he was to walk down there, he would never leave.

**Rick Collignon** is the author of *The Journal of Antonio Montoya, Perdido, A Santo in the Image of Cristóbal Garcia,* and *Madewell Brown*. He lives in northern New Mexico.